MAIGRET
and the
FLEMISH SHOP

Georges Simenon

MAIGRET and the FLEMISH SHOP

Translated from the French
by Geoffrey Sainsbury

A Harvest / HBJ Book
A Helen and Kurt Wolff Book
Harcourt Brace Jovanovich, Publishers
San Diego New York London

HBJ

Library of Congress Cataloging-in-Publication Data
Simenon, Georges, 1903–1989.
[Chez les Flamands. English]
Maigret and the Flemish shop / Georges Simenon;
translated from the French by Geoffrey Sainsbury.
p. cm.
"A Helen and Kurt Wolff book."
ISBN 0-15-655121-7 (pbk.)
I. Title.
PQ2637.I53C4513 1990
843'.912—dc20 89-26879

Printed in the United States of America
First Harvest/HBJ edition 1990
A B C D E

MAIGRET
and the
FLEMISH SHOP

1

Anna Peeters

WHEN Maigret got out of the train at Givet the first person he saw was Anna Peeters.

She was standing exactly opposite his carriage, as though she had foreseen that he would stop just there. Yet she seemed neither surprised nor proud of having calculated so nicely. She looked just the same as when he had seen her in Paris: probably she was never otherwise. Her coat and skirt were iron-gray, her shoes black, while her hat was the kind of thing of which it is absolutely impossible to remember either the color or the shape.

Only one difference. Here, on the almost empty, wind-swept platform, she seemed a shade taller and broader. Her nose was red, and the handkerchief she was holding was rolled up in a ball.

"I felt sure you'd come, *Monsieur le commissaire.*"

She certainly looked sure, but whether she was sure of him or of herself was not so easy to tell. Without any smile of greeting, she asked in a business-like way:

"Have you any other luggage?"

No. Maigret only had his shabby old gladstone-bag, and, heavy as it was, he didn't want a porter.

The few third-class passengers who had left the train had already disappeared. The girl held out her platform ticket to the collector, who stared hard at her. That, however, did not appear to embarrass her, and as soon as they had passed through she went on:

"I thought at first of getting a room ready for you at home. But on second thoughts I decided it would be more suitable for you to be in a hotel. So I booked one of the best rooms in the *Hôtel de la Meuse.*"

They dived into the narrow streets of Givet, where every passer-by turned round to look at them. Maigret walked heavily, his gladstone dragging at his shoulder. He was trying to take everything in, the people in the streets, the houses, and, most of all, his companion.

"What's that noise?" he asked, conscious of a vague murmur that he could not identify.

"The Meuse in flood, pounding against the piles of the bridge. Shipping's been held up for the last three weeks."

At the end of a narrow lane they suddenly found themselves facing the wide river. Here and there, the brown flood spread out over the fields. In other places a shed stood up out of the water.

At least a hundred barges were there, as well as tugs and dredgers, all made fast alongside one another to form one vast floating block.

"Here's your hotel. I'm afraid it's none too comfortable. Perhaps you'd like to stop for a while and have a bath?"

It was bewildering. Maigret did not know what to think of her. Perhaps no woman had ever aroused his curiosity so much as Anna Peeters, who remained perfectly calm, without smiling, without making the slightest attempt to look pretty, and who now and again dabbed her red nose with her handkerchief.

She must have been between twenty-five and thirty. Much taller than the average, she was also a solidly built, large-boned woman to a degree that made anything like gracefulness impossible.

Her clothes were extremely sober and quite commonplace. It was only her bearing that was really quite distinguished. She seemed perfectly at home, and treated Maigret as her guest. It was up to her to make all arrangements.

"I've no reason to want a bath."

"In that case, perhaps you'd come to the house right away. Give your bag to the porter.—Here! Porter! . . . Take it up to No. 9. . . . Monsieur will be coming back presently."

And Maigret, watching her out of the corner of his eye, thought:

"I must look like a schoolboy!"

Yet that was just the absurdity of it: he looked anything but a schoolboy! If she was stoutly built, he was nevertheless half as big again, and his enormous overcoat made him look as though hewn from a block of granite.

"You're not too tired?"

"I'm not tired at all."

"In that case I can run through the principal points as we walk along."

As a matter of fact, she had already been through the principal points in Paris. One day, on entering his room at the *Police Judiciaire*, he had found this stranger, who had been patiently waiting for two or three hours. Nothing the clerk had said had succeeded in choking her off.

When anybody had tried to find out her business, they had only received the answer:

"It's personal."

As soon as the inspector had sat down at his desk, she had handed him a letter. Maigret had at once recognized the writing as that of a cousin of his wife's, living at Nancy.

My dear Maigret,

Mademoiselle Anna Peeters has been recommended to me by my brother-in-law, who knew her ten years ago, and who gives her an excellent character. As for her troubles, she can tell you about them herself. Do what you can for her. . . .

"You live at Nancy?"

"No. Givet."

"But this letter . . ."

"I went on purpose to Nancy, before coming to Paris, for I knew that I could get an introduction to someone high up in the police."

She wasn't like the usual person who came to beg a favor. She didn't fidget, she didn't stumble over her words, she didn't plead. There was nothing pathetic about her, or even humble. Looking straight in front of her, she stated her business clearly, as though claiming no more than her due.

"Unless you take the matter up, we're lost, all of us, and it will be the most horrible mistake."

Maigret had listened attentively to a rather complicated family story.

The Peeters kept a shop by the Belgian frontier. A father and mother, and three children. Anna worked in the shop, Maria was a teacher, while Joseph was a law student at Nancy. . . .

This Joseph had had a child by a local girl. The child was now three years of age. . . . And all at once its mother had disappeared, and the Peeters were suspected of having either killed or kidnapped her. . . .

It had nothing whatever to do with Maigret. The local police were handling the case and had not appealed for help. In fact, when Maigret had wired for information, the answer was in no way ambiguous:

Peeters family guilty stop arrest imminent.

That had decided him. So here he was in Givet, though without any official authority, being led by the hand, so to speak, by Anna Peeters, whom he never stopped observing.

*

The river sped northward, swirling noisily round each pile of the bridge, and carrying whole trees in its onrush.

The wind, sweeping up the valley against the stream, lashed the water into real waves. It was no more than three o'clock, yet the day was already drawing in.

Gusts of wind blew down the streets. The few people in them hurried about their business, and Anna was not the only one whose nose was running.

"Look down this lane. . . . On the left . . ."

Anna paused as discreetly as she could, and with a slight movement of her hand indicated the second house, a poor, two-storied cottage. A window was already lit up by an oil-lamp in one of the rooms.

"That's where she lives."

"Who?"

"Germaine Piedbœuf, of course. The girl who . . ."

"Who had your brother's child?"

"If it's his. We've only her word for it. . . . Look!"

In the doorway of another house, a couple were standing in the shadow. The girl, who wore no hat, was doubtless a factory-hand. Only the man's back was visible.

"Is that her?"

"How could it be? I told you she'd disappeared. . . . But it's one of the same sort. You see what I mean? . . . And she persuaded my brother he was its father."

"Isn't the child like him?"

And Anna answered coldly:

"He's like his mother. Come on. We'd better be going. These people are always spying at you from behind their curtains."

"Does she live with her family?"

"With her father, who's a night-watchman at the factory. And then there's her brother, Gérard."

The little house, and most of all the lamp-lit window, were henceforth engraved on the inspector's mind.

"You've never been to Givet before?"

"I've been through it once, but without stopping."

The quay seemed interminable. It was very wide, and every twenty yards was a bollard for the mooring-ropes of the barges. A few warehouses. A low building, over which a flag was flying.

"That's the French Customs House. . . . We live further on, near the Belgian."

The lighters tugged at their moorings and

rubbed against each other. Some untethered horses were browsing on the few patches of thin grass.

"Do you see that light? . . . That's our house."

A customs officer watched them pass, without saying anything. A group of bargees watched them too, and then began talking in Flemish.

"What are they saying?"

She did not answer at once, and for the first time she turned her head away.

"That one would never know the truth."

And she quickened her pace, leaning forward into the wind.

They had left the town behind them. This was the domain of the river, the customs, barges, and bargees. Here and there an electric light, switched on prematurely, looked weak and thin in the fading afternoon light. Some washing, hung up in one of the barges, flapped noisily in the wind. A few children were playing in the mud.

"The detective came again yesterday. He said the examining magistrate had given orders we were to hold ourselves at the disposal of the police. That's the fourth time they've come and searched the house from top to bottom."

They were approaching the house, a fair-sized building, by the quay, where more barges than usual were made fast alongside. There was no other house near by. Nothing but the Belgian Customs House a hundred yards away, beside which stood a boundary-stone marking the frontier.

"Will you come in?"

On the windows of the door were transparent advertisements of some brand of metal polish. As it opened, a bell rang inside.

And the moment you crossed the threshold you were enveloped in warmth and an indescribable atmosphere, thick and quiet, laden with a mixture of smells. It wasn't easy to sort them out. A trace of cinnamon, and a graver undercurrent of ground coffee. Behind those was kerosene, and lastly a whiff of gin.

A single electric light in the middle of the shop. A counter painted dark brown, across which a white-haired woman in a black bodice was talking in Flemish to a bargee's wife who carried a baby.

"Will you come straight through, Inspector?"

Maigret had time to catch a glimpse of shelves piled high with goods. More especially, he noticed that one part of the counter was covered with zinc and that on it stood bottles of gin or eau-de-vie with tin pouring-spouts.

But he had no time to see more, as he was being shown through another glass-paneled door, fitted with a muslin curtain. They went through the kitchen, where an old man was sitting in a wicker arm-chair, drawn up close to the stove.

"This way."

It was colder in the passage beyond. Then another door, opening onto an unexpected room, half drawing-room, half dining-room, with a piano, a violin-case, a carefully polished parquet floor, comfortable furniture, reproductions of famous pictures on the walls.

"Let me take your overcoat."

The table was laid. A check table-cloth, silver, cups and saucers of fine china.

"You'll have some coffee, won't you?"

Maigret's coat was already hanging in the passage, and Anna returned to the room in a white silk blouse which made her even less girlish than before.

And yet she was a full-bodied woman. What was it, then, that divested her of all femininity? It was impossible to imagine her falling in love. Still more impossible to think of a man falling in love with her.

Obviously everything had been arranged beforehand. She brought in a steaming coffee-pot, and poured out three cupfuls. Disappearing again for a moment, she returned with a *tarte au riz*.

"Sit down, *Monsieur le commissaire*. . . . My mother will be coming in a moment."

"Is it you who plays the piano?"

"And my sister too. But she has less time than I have. In the evening she generally has some exercises to correct."

"And the violin?"

"That's my brother's."

"He's not in Givet, I suppose?"

"He'll be here presently. I told him you were coming."

She cut the tart and handed Maigret a slice with such authority that there was no question of his refusing. Madame Peeters entered the room, her hands clasped in front of her, greeting the guest with a timid smile, a smile full of sadness and resignation.

"Anna told me you were coming. It's very kind of you. . . ."

She was more Flemish than her daughter, and she spoke with a decided accent. Her features, however, were of considerable refinement, and her strikingly white hair invested her with a certain distinction. She sat on the edge of her chair, like a woman who never sits for more than a few minutes at a time.

"You must be hungry after your journey. For my part, I've lost all appetite since . . ."

Maigret thought of the old man by the kitchen stove. Why didn't he come for a cup of coffee and a slice of tart? At the same moment Madame Peeters said to her daughter:

"Take a slice to your father."

And to the inspector:

"He hardly ever leaves his chair. In fact, he doesn't realize . . ."

The atmosphere was so far from being dramatic that it was hard to believe that anything could disturb it. The impression one had on entering was that even the most fearsome events outside could make little headway against the peace and quiet of this Flemish house, where there was not a particle of dust, not a breath of air, and no sound but the gentle snoring of the stove.

And Maigret, while starting on his thick slice of tart, began asking questions.

"When did it happen, exactly?"

"On January 3rd."

"And it's now the 20th."

"Yes. They didn't think of accusing us at the beginning."

"This girl—what do you call her? Germaine . . ."

"Germaine Piedbœuf," answered Anna, who was now back in the room. "She came about eight in the evening. My mother went into the shop to see what she wanted."

"What did she want?"

Madame Peeters brushed away a tear as she answered:

"The same as usual. . . . She complained that Joseph never came to see her or even sent her a word. . . . And to think of all the work he has to do! It's wonderful how he does it, with all this trouble hanging over our heads. . . ."

"Did she stay long?"

"About five minutes, I suppose. I had to tell her not to shout, as we didn't want all the bargees coming in to see what was the matter. Then Anna came into the shop and told her she'd better go."

"And she went?"

"Anna led her out, while I came back into the kitchen and went on clearing the table."

"You never saw her again?"

"Never."

"In fact, from that moment she wasn't seen again by anybody?"

"That's what they say."

"Had she said anything about suicide?"

"No. And girls of that sort don't kill themselves. . . . Won't you have some more coffee? . . . And another bit of tart? Anna made it. . . ."

The latter sat placidly on her chair. She watched the inspector as though the rôles were reversed, as though it was she who belonged to the Quai des Orfèvres and he to the Flemish shop.

"What were you all doing that evening? Can you remember?"

It was with a sad smile that Anna answered:

"We've had to remember! They've questioned us over and over again. Coming back from the shop, I went upstairs to fetch some knitting-wool. My sister was here playing the piano. When I came down, Marguerite had just arrived."

"Marguerite?"

"A cousin, the daughter of Dr. Van de Weert. They live in Givet. . . . And I may as well tell you at once—you're bound to know sooner or later—she's engaged to Joseph."

Madame Peeters got up with a sigh, as the shop bell had rung. Then she could be heard talking Flemish in the shop in an almost cheerful voice while weighing out some haricots or peas.

"It's been a terrible grief to my mother. Ever since they were tiny, it's been an understood thing that they were to be married. At sixteen they were definitely engaged. But of course there was no question of marriage till Joseph was through with the University. . . . Then this child came. . . ."

"And it made a difference, I suppose?"

"Yes. Only Marguerite was determined she'd never marry anyone else. She and Joseph have always loved each other."

"Did Germaine Piedbœuf know about her?"

"Yes. But she'd made up her mind to marry Joseph, and she got at him, until in the end, for peace' sake, he promised. In fact, the wedding was to be as soon as he passed his exams."

The shop bell rang again, and Madame Peeters trotted back to the sitting-room.

"You were telling me what you did on the evening of the 3rd."

"Yes, and as I said, I came downstairs and found Marguerite and my sister in this room. . . . We were playing the piano most of the time up to about half-past ten. My father went to bed as usual at nine. Then, when Marguerite went, my sister and I accompanied her as far as the bridge."

"Did you meet anybody?"

"Nobody. . . . It was very cold. . . . We came home, and the next day we went on just as usual without suspecting anything had happened. In the afternoon something was said about Germaine Piedbœuf's having disappeared. The day after, it looked serious; but it wasn't till the day after that that we realized we had come under suspicion because the girl had come to the shop. We had to go and make statements to the police, and they searched the whole premises. They even did some digging in the garden."

"Your brother wasn't in Givet on the 3rd?"

"No, he only comes at week-ends. Very rarely

during the week. He rides over on his motor-bike. . . . Everybody's against us. The whole town. You see, we're foreigners . . . and we've more money than most."

A note of pride came into her voice. Or rather a note of self-assurance.

"You've no idea of all the dreadful things they've been saying. . . ."

The shop bell rang again, then a youthful voice called out:

"It's only me."

Hurried steps, and a moment later Marguerite burst into the sitting-room, halting abruptly at the sight of Maigret.

"Excuse me. . . . I didn't know . . ."

"It's Inspector Maigret. . . . You know. . . . He's come to help us."

Then, turning to Maigret:

"This is my cousin."

A tiny, gloved hand was enclosed in the inspector's heavy paw. A shy smile.

"Yes. Anna told me you were coming."

Marguerite was a very feminine type. Small and well-cut features surrounded by fair, curly hair.

"I hear you play the piano."

"Yes. I love music more than anything . . . particularly if I'm sad."

Her smile made one think of the pretty faces of advertisements, the lips slightly pouting, the eyes soft, the head a little inclined.

"Isn't Maria here yet?"

"No. Her train must be late."

Maigret was sitting on a thin-legged chair that creaked as he crossed his legs.

"At what time did you come here on the evening of the 3rd?"

"About half-past eight. We always have dinner early, and that night my father had some friends coming in afterwards to play bridge."

"What was the weather like?"

"It was raining and very cold. It rained all that week."

"Was the river already in flood?"

"It was rising rapidly. But the weirs hadn't been carried away then, and the boats were still going up and down."

"A little more tart, Inspector? . . . Are you sure you won't? . . . A cigar, then?"

Anna held out a box of Belgian cigars, explaining:

"They're not smuggled. You see, half the house is in Belgium and the other half in France."

"One thing: they can't drag your brother in, can they? He was at Nancy, I suppose?"

Anna frowned.

"I'm afraid it's not so simple as that. Only the other day a drunken sot came forward and told the police he'd seen Joseph's motor-bike pass along the quay. As if he could remember a thing like that all of a sudden a fortnight later! . . . It's another bit of Gérard's wangling—he's Germaine Piedbœuf's brother. That's about all he has to do—running round trying to trump up evidence against us. The Piedbœufs are out to make a good thing out of this. In fact, we've heard they want to claim three hundred thousand francs damages."

"Where's the child?"

They could hear Madame Peeters hurrying from the kitchen into the shop, where the bell had rung once more. Anna put the tart away in the sideboard and stood the coffee-pot on the stove.

"At home with them."

A raucous voice came from the shop. A bargee ordering a glass of gin.

2

"L'Etoile Polaire"

WITH nervous fingers Marguerite Van de Weert was rummaging in her handbag. She was obviously in a hurry to show something.

"You haven't seen the *Echo de Givet,* have you?"

She handed a newspaper-cutting to Anna while a modest smile played about her lips.

"Who gave you the idea?" asked Anna.

"Nobody. I suddenly thought of it."

Anna passed the cutting on to Maigret. It was only an advertisement.

A substantial reward will be paid if the motorcyclist who passed along the Meuse road on the evening of the 3rd will present himself at the Epicerie Peeters, *Givet.*

"I didn't dare give my address, but I thought . . ."

It seemed to Maigret that Anna looked at her cousin a trifle impatiently, while she murmured:

"Certainly. . . . It's an idea. . . . But nobody'll come."

Poor Marguerite, who had so much looked forward to the applause which would greet her maneuver!

"Why shouldn't anybody come? If somebody went by on a motor-bike, why shouldn't he come forward? We know it wasn't Joseph. . . ."

The sitting-room door was open, and they could hear the kettle singing in the kitchen, where Madame Peeters was busying herself with the dinner. And voices too, coming from the entrance of the shop. The two girls at once pricked their ears.

"Come in, will you? I don't suppose we've anything to tell you, but . . ."

"Joseph!" stammered Marguerite, rising from her chair.

It was not so much love as fervor that animated her voice and transfigured her. In obvious suspense, she remained standing, waiting for her fiancé to appear. And everything about her promised the appearance of some superman.

His voice reached them again, coming this time from the kitchen:

"Good evening, Mother. . . ."

And a stranger's voice:

"I hope you'll excuse me, madame, but I've a few small points to check, and seeing your son pass . . ."

The two newcomers were now in the sitting-room doorway. At the sight of Marguerite, Joseph frowned ever so slightly.

"How are you, Marguerite?" he said, with a forced gentleness that was a little embarrassing.

She took his hand in both of hers.

"You're not too tired, Joseph? . . . You mustn't let this get you down."

Anna, more self-possessed, had turned to the other person.

"This is Inspector Maigret here. Perhaps you already know him . . . ?"

"Machère," answered the man, introducing himself. "Is it true that you . . . ?"

They were all somehow uncomfortable, cluttered up as they were between the door and the table.

"I'm here quite unofficially," grunted Maigret. "Please go on exactly as you would if I wasn't here."

He felt a touch on his arm.

"My brother, Joseph. . . . Inspector Maigret."

Joseph held out a long, cold, bony hand. He was half a head taller than Maigret, though the latter was tall enough at five foot eleven. But he was so slightly built that, in spite of his twenty-five years, he gave the impression of a growing boy.

A pinched nose. Tired eyes with dark rings under them. Fair hair cut very short. He must have had weak eyes too, for he was constantly blinking, as though to ward off the light.

"Enchanté, Monsieur le commissaire. . . ."

There wasn't even any style about him. When

he took off his greasy mackintosh it was to disclose a poorly cut, nondescript gray suit.

"I caught sight of him by the bridge," said the detective, Machère. "So I asked him to give me a lift on his carrier."

Then he turned to Anna, addressing her as if she was the real mistress of the house. Madame Peeters was in the kitchen with her husband, who had not stirred from his wicker chair by the stove.

"I suppose there's a way up onto the roof?"

Glances were exchanged.

"By the little window in the loft," answered Anna. "Do you want to go up?"

"Yes. I'd just like to have a look."

It gave Maigret an opportunity to look over the house. The stairs were covered with linoleum, so polished that you had to be careful not to slip.

Three doors gave on to the first-floor landing. Marguerite and Joseph had remained downstairs. Anna led the way, and Maigret noticed a slight roll of her hips as she walked.

"I'd like to have a word with you," whispered Machère.

"Presently."

They reached the second floor. One side had been converted into an attic room. The other, left as it was, with the rafters showing, was used as a storeroom. To reach the little window, Machère had to climb on to a couple of packing-cases.

"Have you got a light?" asked Maigret.

"A flash-light. . . ."

He was young, with a round jovial face. Obviously a man of tireless energy. Maigret did not follow him out on to the roof, but watched through the little window. The wind blew in squalls. He could hear the dull roar of the river and see on its ruffled surface the broken reflection of the lights on the other bank.

To the left, on the cornice, stood a 400-gallon tank of galvanized iron, whose purpose was to collect rain-water. The detective made straight for it.

He looked into it, but was apparently disappointed, for he turned away at once. He then walked for a moment or two on the roof, suddenly stooping down to pick something up.

Maigret withdrew his head, to find Anna waiting patiently behind him. A second later Machère's legs appeared, then his body and head.

"I hadn't thought of it till this afternoon, though I knew people drank rain-water here. . . . But the body's not there."

"What was it you picked up?"

"A handkerchief. A lady's handkerchief."

He spread it out and turned his flash-light on it, but looked in vain for a monogram. The handkerchief was filthy, having no doubt been there, exposed to the weather, for some time.

"We must look into this," said Machère as he turned to go.

*

Returning to the warmth of the sitting-room, they found Joseph sitting on the piano-stool, reading the advertisement which Marguerite had just shown him. She stood before him in her smart and very feminine clothes.

"Would you like to come along with me?" Maigret asked the young detective.

"Where are you staying?"

"The *Hôtel de la Meuse,*" answered Anna. "But are you going already, Inspector? . . . I was hoping you'd stay to dinner. But of course . . . I don't want to press you. . . ."

Maigret crossed the kitchen, Madame Peeters looking at him aghast.

"Are you going?"

As for the old man, his eyes were devoid of any sparkle of intelligence. He smoked away at his meerschaum pipe, his thoughts, if he had any, on it alone. Not the faintest notice did he take of Maigret.

They were outside now in the wind, with the roar of the river and the bumping of the boats. Machère found himself on Maigret's right, but he quickly shifted to the other side in deference to his superior.

"Do you think they're innocent?"

"I've no idea. Have you got any tobacco?"

"I'm afraid not. . . . You know, they've been talking about you a lot at Nancy. And that's what bothers me. Because these Peeters . . ."

But Maigret had stopped and was gazing at the boats in the stream. Thanks to the stoppage of traffic on the river, Givet had quite the look of a big port. There were several Rhine lighters of a thousand tons—great black things of steel. Beside them the wooden barges from the north looked like varnished toys.

"I shall have to buy a cap," grumbled Maigret, whose hand was glued to the brim of his bowler.

"What did they tell you?" asked Machère. "That they were innocent, of course!"

He had to shout to make himself heard above the wind. Givet, five hundred yards away, was just a cluster of lights. Behind them the Flemish house rose into the boisterous sky, its windows yellowed by gentle light.

"Where do they come from?"

"From the north of Belgium. The old man was born somewhere up beyond Limbourg by the Dutch frontier. . . . He's twenty years older than his wife, and has turned eighty. He was a basket-maker with four men under him, working in the workshop behind the house. It's not many years since he gave it up. But he's completely senile now."

"They're moneyed people?"

"They're supposed to be. The house is theirs and they've been known to advance money to bargees with no capital, to enable them to buy a barge of their own. . . . They're not quite the same as us. A different outlook. By all accounts they're worth hundreds of thousands of francs, but that doesn't stop the old lady serving slugs of gin over the counter. Only, of course, the son's to be a lawyer. The daughters play the piano, and one's a *régente* in a big convent in Namur. . . . That's more than an ordinary teacher. Something like being mistress in a *lycée*."

Machère pointed to the barges.

"Half the men in them are Flemish. And they don't like changing their habits, particularly in the matter of drink. The French bargees go to the bars down by the bridge, but the Belgians won't go without their native gin if they can help it. And they like to be served by people who talk their own language. Besides, being astride of the frontier, the Peeters can sell French and Belgian goods alike. That's a great advantage. Often enough a boat will take in stocks for a week or more. That's good business, I can tell you."

The wind pressed their overcoats against their legs. It was so rough that spray was being flicked on to the decks of the laden barges.

"They've got queer ideas. It makes a difference to them that the place isn't exactly a bar. You can have a drink there, but it remains a grocer's all the same; and the women have a slug too as they do their shopping. . . . It's the drink that pays best, yet the Peeters would never admit they kept a bar."

"The Piedbœufs?"

"A different stamp altogether. . . . A night-watchman in the factory. The daughter was a typist in the same business. The boy works there too."

"Is he a steady chap?"

"It's difficult to say, but I doubt it. He doesn't

seem to put in a great deal of work, judging by the time he spends playing billiards at the *Café de la Mairie*. . . . He's a good-looking fellow, and knows it."

"And his sister?"

"Germaine? . . . She's knocked about with plenty of young fellows. You know: the sort you find kissing in any dark corner. . . . Still there's no doubt about one thing: the child is Joseph Peeters' all right. I've seen it, and nobody could say it wasn't like him. . . . And then, of course—one always comes back to the same point—Germaine went to the shop on the evening of the 3rd, and not a soul has seen her since."

Machère was not afraid of speaking his mind.

"I've searched high and low. I even got an architect to help me, and we made plans of the house to scale. There was only that one thing that I forgot—the roof. . . . In the ordinary way, one would hardly think of a body being hidden on a roof. That's why I came back this afternoon. . . . I found the handkerchief, but nothing else."

"What about the Meuse?"

"Exactly! I was coming to that. I expect you know that when people are drowned the bodies are nearly always recovered at the weirs. There are ten of them between Givet and Namur. But these floods came, and the whole lot of them were carried away. That was two or three days after the crime. . . . It's about time they did something about it, for it happens almost every winter. But there it is! And if Germaine Pied-bœuf's body was chucked into the river, there's no reason why it shouldn't be in Holland by now, or right out in the open sea."

"I was told that Joseph wasn't here that evening."

"I know. That's what he says. But there's a witness who claims to have recognized his motor-bike here at Givet."

"Has the boy any alibi?"

"He gives quite a plausible account of himself, but there's nothing to corroborate it. He lives in lodgings where he can easily get in and out without anybody seeing him. He says he spent most of the evening in one of the bars frequented by students. I went over to Nancy and questioned a number of them. Several can remember his spending an evening with them, but not one of them can be sure whether it was the 3rd, the 4th, or the 5th."

"Any chance of its being suicide?"

"Precious little. She wasn't the type. A common little thing, with not much health and no morals. . . . But she doted on the child."

"Is there nobody else in the picture?"

Machère did not answer immediately. His eye wandered to the barges, which formed a little island, separated from the land by a few yards of water.

"I've tried myself to think of anybody else who might have done it," he went on at last.

"I've checked up on all the bargees. . . . Most of them are a very steady lot, who live on board with their wives and children.

"There was only one boat I didn't like the look of. Absolutely filthy, and in such rotten condition that it's a wonder she keeps afloat. The *Etoile Polaire,* the last boat upstream."

"Whose is it?"

"A Belgian's. Comes from Tilleur near Liége. He's a nasty old brute who's been had up before for assaulting girls. He won't spend a sou on upkeep, and there isn't a company that will insure his boat. . . . Apart from the time he was had up, there have been any amount of stories of the way he carries on with women and little girls. . . . But there's nothing whatever to connect him with Germaine Piedbœuf."

The two men walked on towards the bridge. They came to street lamps, then bars on the right, French bars with automatic pianos.

"I'm keeping an eye on him all the same. . . . But this evidence about the motor-bike . . ."

"Where are you staying?"

"At the *Hôtel de la Gare.*"

Maigret held out his hand.

"I'll be seeing you again, old man. . . . In the meantime, don't forget, you're in charge of the case. I'm only here as an amateur."

"But what do you expect me to do about it? . . . If we don't find the body, we'll never be able to prove anything. And if it's been thrown in the water, we never will find it. . . ."

Maigret shook hands with him absent-mindedly and walked off to the *Hôtel de la Meuse.*

*

During dinner Maigret had written in his little notebook:

Opinions on the Peeters.

Machère: It's the drink that pays best, but they'd never admit they kept a bar.

Landlord of Hôtel de la Meuse: *They take themselves very seriously. It never occurred to me to make* my *son into a lawyer.*

A bargee: In Belgium they're all like that.

Another: They stand up for each other like a band of Free Masons.

At the bridge you were right in the heart of a small French town. Little streets. Cafés full of people playing billiards and dominoes. The smell of aniseed, rising from the *apéritifs*.

Then that short stretch of river, the customs houses, and finally the Flemish shop that was at once the last house in France and the first in Belgium. A Flemish shop whose shelves were bent under the weight of food-stuffs; a bit of counter covered with zinc for the gin-drinkers; a kitchen behind, where a man turned eighty sat aimlessly in his wicker chair by the stove; a general living-room with a piano, a violin, comfortable chairs, a home-made tart, the large checks of the table-cloth. Then Anna and Marguerite, and Joseph, tall and weedy, arriving on his motor-bike to be admired by his womenfolk.

The *Hôtel de la Meuse* was a commercial hotel. The landlord knew all the travelers, each of whom had his own napkin.

About nine o'clock Joseph Peeters slunk in timidly, went up to the inspector, and stammered:

"Have you . . . have you heard the news?"

Everyone turned to stare at them, so Maigret thought it better to take the young man up to his room.

"What is it?"

"You knew about the advertisement, didn't you? . . . Well, a chap's come forward, a garage-hand from Dinant, who says he passed along the road by the Meuse about half-past eight on his motor-bike. He remembers passing our house."

Maigret hadn't started unpacking. He sat on the bed, leaving the only arm-chair to his visitor.

"Do you really love Marguerite?"

"Yes . . . that is . . ."

"That is what?"

"She's a cousin of ours. We were engaged to be married. It was decided ages ago."

"But it didn't stop you having an affair with Germaine Piedbœuf."

A silence. Then a faintly muttered:

"No."

"Did you love her?"

"I don't know."

"Would you have married her?"

"I don't know."

The light shone full on Joseph's thin face, with its tired eyes and sagging features. He didn't dare look Maigret in the face.

"How did it happen?"

"I came across her. Started knocking about with her . . ."

"And Marguerite?"

"That's different altogether."

"And then?"

"Then she said she was going to have a baby. I didn't know what to do. . . ."

"It was your mother who . . . ?"

"Yes, and my sisters. They persuaded me that Germaine had already had other . . ."

"Other adventures? . . ."

The window looked out on to the river just where it was broken by the piles of the bridge. The din was incessant.

"Do you love Marguerite?"

The young man stood up, anxious, ill at ease.

"What do you mean?"

"Are you in love with Marguerite or Germaine?"

"I . . . As a matter of fact . . ."

There were beads of sweat on his forehead.

"How should I know? . . . My mother had already made plans to set me up as a lawyer in Rheims."

"Plans for you and Marguerite. Is that it?"

"I suppose so. . . . I met the other at a dance."

"Germaine?"

"At a dance I was forbidden to go to. . . . I saw her home. . . . And on the way . . ."

"And Marguerite?"

"That's different altogether. . . . I . . ."

"You didn't leave Nancy on the night of the 3rd?"

Maigret had had enough. He moved towards the door. He had sized Joseph up: raw-boned but spineless. His self-respect was only just maintained by the admiration of his sisters and cousin.

"What are you doing with yourself these days?"

"Working for my exam. It's the last. . . . Anna sent me a telegram asking me to run over and see you. . . . Do you . . . ?"

"No, I don't need you here. You can go back to Nancy."

A figure that Maigret was not to forget for many a long day. Blinking eyes that had become red-rimmed with worry. The jacket cut too straight. The trousers baggy at the knees.

In the same suit, with a mackintosh slipped over it, he would soon be riding off to Nancy, without exceeding the speed limits in the villages.

And at Nancy he would find a typical little student's bedroom with an obliging old landlady to look after him. . . . Lectures that he never cut. . . . At noon the café. . . . Billiards in the evening. . . .

"If I want you, I'll let you know."

And Maigret, left alone, put his elbows on the window-sill and gazed once more at the Meuse rushing down towards the lowlands. In the distance a quiet little light: the Flemish shop.

On the dark surface of the water, still darker masses. Boats, masts, funnels, the blunt bows of the barges.

Nearest of all, the *Etoile Polaire*.

He went out, filling his pipe, with his coat collar turned up. And the wind was so strong that, in spite of his weight, he had to lean forward to keep his balance.

3
The Photograph

As usual, Maigret was up and about at eight o'clock. With his hands in his overcoat pockets and his pipe between his teeth, he stood motionless, his eye resting sometimes on the racing river, sometimes on the passers-by.

The wind was just as strong as on the previous day. It was much colder than in Paris.

He was standing on French soil, yet it was impossible to forget the nearness of the frontier. The houses were definitely Belgian houses, of ugly brown brick, with doorsteps of hewn stone, and copper flower-pots on the window-sills.

The people, too, had in their lined faces something of the hardness of the Walloon type. And then there was the khaki uniform of the Belgian customs officers.

Givet was unmistakably a frontier town, the

meeting-ground of two nations. Even in the shops you could not forget it, as both French and Belgian money were accepted.

Mairgret was more than ever conscious of it when he went into one of the *bistros* on the quay for a glass of hot grog. A typical French *bistro*, with the whole range of *apéritifs* of all colors. Light-colored walls, covered with mirrors.

Some ten or a dozen bargees were standing at the bar, having their morning glass of white wine, talking to the owners of a couple of tugs. They were discussing the possibility of proceeding downstream in spite of the floods.

"It's doubtful whether you'd get under the bridge at Dinant. And even if you could, we're asking fifteen francs a ton per kilometer."

"It's too much. . . . At that price it's best to hang on."

Eyes were turned on Maigret. One of them, spotting who he was, nudged his neighbor.

"One of the Belgians is talking of going down without a tug at all. Just drifting down the stream. . . ."

There wasn't a single Belgian in the café. They preferred the Peeters' shop with its dark woodwork and its mingled smells of coffee, chicory, cinnamon, and gin. There, in their own atmosphere, they could stand for hours at a time, leaning on the counter, talking lazily, while their blue eyes would stare dreamily at the transparent advertisements stuck on the glass door.

Maigret listened to all that was said around him.

From the conversation, he gathered that the Belgians were unpopular, not so much because they differed in character, as because they were competitors. Their boats were kept in a perfect state of repair and were fitted with powerful motors, and they were generally in a position to undercut the French, often accepting cargoes at rates which the latter thought ridiculous.

"And they go about killing girls into the bargain!"

The remark was made for Maigret's benefit, and the speaker watched the inspector out of the corner of his eye.

"Why don't they arrest the whole family? I can't think what the police are waiting for. . . . Unless it's because they're well-to-do folk. . . ."

Maigret left the bar and wandered once more along the quay, watching the brown flood which swept branches of trees down towards the sea. In a little side-street on the left he suddenly caught sight of the house which Anna had pointed out to him.

The morning light was grim, the sky a uniform gray. The people in the streets were cold, and hurried about their business.

Maigret went up to the front door and gave a pull at the bell. It was a little after a quarter past eight. The woman who opened the door had apparently been washing or scrubbing, for she wiped her hands on her wet apron as she asked:

"What do you want?"

At the end of the passage he could see the

kitchen, and in the middle of the floor a pail and a scrubbing-brush.

"Is Monsieur Piedbœuf in?"

The woman looked him up and down mistrustfully.

"Which Monsieur Piedbœuf?"

"The father."

"You're from the police, I suppose. In that case, you ought to know that he's always in bed at this time of the morning. He's on duty all night and only comes off at seven. . . . Still, if you'd like to go up . . ."

"I won't disturb him, thank you. What about his son?"

"He went out to work ten minutes ago."

Maigret heard a spoon drop on to the kitchen floor, and looking over the woman's shoulder he could see a bit of a child's head.

"Is that, by any chance . . . ?" he began.

"Yes, that's poor Mademoiselle Germaine's boy. . . . Well, are you coming in or not? If you stand in the doorway much longer you'll make the whole house cold."

Maigret went in. The passage walls were painted imitation marble. The kitchen was in a fearful mess, and the woman muttered under her breath as she removed the pail. But it was impossible to tell whether she was grumbling or apologizing.

On the table were dirty cups and plates. A child of two was sitting all alone, clumsily eating a boiled egg and smearing his chin with the yolk.

The woman was at least forty. She was thin, and her face ascetic.

"Are you looking after the child?"

"As much as I can. . . . His grandfather's in bed half the day, and there's nobody else at home, now that they've killed his mother. When I'm called out, I take him round to one of the neighbors."

"When you're called out?"

"Yes. I'm a certified midwife."

She had discarded her check apron, as though it deprived her of her professional dignity.

"That's all right, my little Jojo, there's nothing to be frightened about."

The child had stopped eating and was staring at the inspector.

Was he really like Joseph Peeters! It was difficult to say. One thing was certain: he was not a robust child. The features were irregular, the head too big, the neck thin, and, most striking of all, the mouth was long and thin and looked like a ten-year-old's, to say the least of it.

He stared on at the inspector, but the eyes expressed nothing. Nor did any expression come into them when the midwife thought fit to kiss him rather theatrically and say:

"Mon pauvre chou! Eat up your egg, *mon chéri!"*

She hadn't asked Maigret to sit down. There was a large pool of water on the floor, and some soup simmering on the stove.

"I suppose you're the person they've brought from Paris?"

The voice was not exactly aggressive, but it was far from being friendly.

"What do you mean?"

"There's no use pretending. Everybody knows about it."

"About what?"

"You know as well as I do. That's a nice job you've put your hand to. . . . But I suppose the police will always be on the same side as there's money!"

Maigret frowned, not because the words had got under his skin, but because of the state of mind they revealed.

"They said as much themselves, those Belgians. They said things might go against them for the moment, but that everything would be changed as soon as some grand inspector came from Paris."

She was aggressive enough now, and her smile was decidedly unpleasant.

"You've only to look, to see how it's done. The case drags on, and the people who ought to be under lock and key are given plenty of time to work out a story amongst themselves. . . . And of course they know very well that Germaine's body will never be found.—Eat up your breakfast, my treasure. There's nothing to be frightened of."

Her eyes moistened as she looked at the child, whose spoon remained in mid-air as he gazed at the intruder.

"There's nothing you'd like to tell me?" asked Maigret.

"Nothing at all. The Peeters will have told you all about everything, and even proved that the child has nothing to do with that Joseph of theirs."

Maigret had been set down as an enemy, and there was nothing to be done about it. The atmosphere of the house was made up of poverty and hatred.

"And if you want to see Monsieur Piedbœuf, you've only to come back about twelve. That's when he gets up. And you'd find Monsieur Gérard here too, as he comes home for lunch."

She led him along the passage and closed the door behind him. Upstairs the blinds were down.

*

Maigret found Machère near the Flemish shop talking to a couple of bargees, whom he left as soon as he caught sight of the inspector.

"What do they say?"

"I was asking them about the *Etoile Polaire*. . . . They think the skipper was at the *Café des Mariniers* on the evening of the 3rd, and that he left about eight, drunk, the same as any other evening. . . . He must be still asleep now, as I was on board a moment ago and he didn't seem to hear me."

Through the shop window they could see Madame Peeters' white hair. She was watching the two policemen as they stood there looking round them and pursuing a desultory conversation.

On one side of them the river that had burst its dams and was coursing along at a good four and a half knots.

On the other side the Flemish shop.

"There are two entrances," said Machère. "The one you can see from where you are, and another at the back. . . . There's a well in the yard. . . ."

And he hastily added:

"I took soundings, and there was no sign of the body there. . . . All the same—though I really can't tell you why—I've got the feeling it wasn't thrown into the Meuse. . . . I'd like to know what that handkerchief was doing on the roof. . . ."

"Did you hear about the motor-cyclist?"

"Yes. But if he did come along this way, it doesn't prove that Joseph didn't."

Exactly! And it was like that all along the line. No proof one way or the other. In fact, no serious evidence at all.

Germaine Piedbœuf came into the shop about eight o'clock. According to the Belgians, she left a few minutes later, but nobody else saw her leave.

She had never been seen again.

And that was pretty well the whole story.

Yet on the strength of it the Piedbœufs were going to claim three hundred thousand francs damages.

Two bargees' wives entered the shop, ringing the bell as they did so.

"Do you still think, Inspector . . . ?"

"I don't think anything at all, old man. I'll be seeing you presently. . . ."

He too went into the shop, the two customers standing aside to make room for him. Madame Peeters called out:

"Anna!"

She bustled over to the kitchen door and opened it.

"Go straight through, *Monsieur le commissaire*. You know your way. . . . Anna'll be down in a moment. She's upstairs doing the rooms. . . ."

She then turned towards her customers, while the inspector went through the kitchen into the passage and slowly climbed the stairs.

Anna had evidently not heard. Sounds were coming from one of the rooms, and looking in through an open door, Maigret saw her, her hair tied up in a kerchief, brushing a pair of trousers.

She caught sight of the visitor in a looking-glass, and turned suddenly, dropping the brush.

"Is that you?"

Though dressed for housework, she looked just the same—well brought up, a little prim and reserved.

"Excuse me! Your mother told me you were up here. . . . Is this your brother's room?"

"Yes. He went off early this morning. He's gone back to his work. There's a stiff exam before him, and he's determined to pass with distinction, as he has in all the others."

On a chest of drawers was a large framed photograph of Marguerite Van de Weert.

And on it the girl had written in a long pointed hand the opening lines of the *Song of Solveig:*

> *L'hiver peut s'enfuir*
> *Le printemps bien-aimé*
> *Peut s'écouler.*

Maigret had picked up the photograph to read the words. Anna looked hard at him—a defensive look, as though she expected him to smile.

"It's by Ibsen," she said.

"I know."

And Maigret even finished the verse:

> *"Moi je t'attends ici,*
> *O mon beau fiancé,*
> *Jusqu'à mon jour dernier."*

He almost smiled, all the same, as his eye fell on the trousers which Anna was still holding. Such high-sounding words in such a homely setting!

And to think of Joseph Peeters, thin and weedy, badly dressed, with fair hair that no amount of brilliantine could keep in place. Joseph Peeters with his weak, blinking eyes and a nose that was out of proportion to the rest. Joseph Peeters. . . .

> *O mon beau fiancé . . .*

And this portrait of a fluffy, pretty-pretty, provincial girl.

What had this quotation to do with Ibsen's tremendous drama? Was it a profession of faith, a flag nailed to a mast? Nothing of the kind! Just a few lines of poetry dutifully copied out by a proper young lady because it was the right thing to do.

Moi je t'attends ici. . . .

That was true, at any rate. She certainly had waited, waited for years. And in spite of Germaine Piedbœuf. In spite of the child.

Maigret felt slightly uncomfortable. He stared at the table covered with green blotting-paper, at the brass ink-stand, which must have been a present, and at the pen-holders made of bakelite.

Absent-mindedly he opened a drawer.

A collection of amateur snapshots lay in a lidless cardboard box.

"My brother has a camera."

Maigret turned them over. . . . A group of lads in student caps. . . . Joseph on his motorbike, leaning forward, his hand on the throttle, looking as though he'd be off in a moment at sixty miles an hour. . . . Anna at the piano. . . . Another girl, more slenderly built with a slight melancholy expression. . . .

"That's my sister, Maria."

And suddenly one that might have been a passport photograph, horrible as all such photos are with their harshly contrasting lights and shades.

A girl who had obviously reached womanhood, yet was so small and frail that the word woman seemed quite inapplicable. Great eyes which devoured half her face. She was wearing an absurd hat and looked as if she was scared by the camera.

"That's Germaine, isn't it?"

Her son was like her.

"Was she ill?"

"She wasn't strong. In fact, I think she'd had a touch of consumption at one time."

Just the opposite of Anna, who was strong as a horse. She was tall and well-knit. Yet what characterized her more than that was a sort of stability, both physical and moral, that was positively staggering. She had at last put the trousers down on the bed, which was covered with a white counterpane.

"I've been to her house."

"What did they say? . . . I expect they . . ."

"I only saw the midwife . . . and the child."

Anna asked no further questions, as though held back by a sudden delicacy.

"Is your room next to this?"

"Yes. My sister and I share it."

There was a door from one room to the other, and the inspector went through. The sisters' room was lighter, as it looked onto the quay. The bed was made; everything was as tidy as could be; not a single article of clothing left lying about—unless you counted the two nightgowns neatly folded on the pillows.

"You're twenty-five, aren't you?"

"Twenty-six."

Maigret wanted to ask her a question, but he didn't know quite how to put it.

"You've never been engaged?" he asked finally.

"Never."

But that wasn't really what he'd wanted to ask her. He was still more intrigued by her now that he'd seen her room. She impressed him like an enigmatic statue. And what he wanted to know was whether this well-made but somewhat forbidding body had ever quickened and quivered, whether this practical girl had ever been anything but a model daughter, a devoted sister, a capable housewife, a Peeters. . . . In other words, whether beneath all that there was a woman.

She didn't shrink. She didn't look away. She must have known his eyes were taking stock of her figure as much as of her face, yet she didn't turn a hair.

"We see very few people. Hardly anybody except our cousins the Van de Weerts. . . ."

Maigret hesitated, and when he did speak his voice wasn't quite natural.

"I want you to help me with a little experiment. . . . Will you go down to the sitting-room and play the piano until I call? And if possible, I'd like you to play what was played on the evening of the 3rd. Who was playing then?"

"Maria was when Germaine came. But Marguerite came in a little later and she took her place. She sings, and plays her own accompaniments. . . . She's had singing lessons."

"What was it she was singing?"

"The thing you saw just now. The *Song of Solveig*. . . . But . . . I . . . I don't understand."

"It's just a little experiment."

She backed out of the room and was going to shut the door.

"No. Leave it open, please."

A minute or two later her fingers were running easily over the keys. Rippling chords floated up the stairs. And Maigret, without losing a moment, began opening the cupboards in the girls' room.

The first contained underclothes. Neat piles of chemises, knickers, and beautifully ironed petticoats.

She had started on the piece now. He recognized the tune. And Maigret's thick fingers felt their way into the piles of white linen.

An onlooker would have taken him for a lover. Or someone racked by a strange hidden passion.

Thick, heavy linen, the kind that wears for ever. No frills, no nonsense.

The next thing was a drawer containing garters, hairpins and such-like. . . . There was no sign anywhere of powder or perfumes, except for a bottle of Russian eau-de-Cologne which was no doubt reserved for grand occasions.

The music swelled until the house seemed full of it. And little by little a voice became audible, growing in volume till finally it dominated the accompaniment:

"Moi je t'attends ici,
O mon beau fiancé . . ."

It wasn't Marguerite's voice that sang those words. It was Anna's. The syllables were distinct. Certain passages were lingered over.

And Maigret's fingers felt and felt.

In another pile of underclothes there was a rustle which was not of linen, but paper.

Another photograph. An amateur snapshot in sepia. A young curly-haired man with well-cut features. The upper lip protruded slightly in a self-confident smile with a touch of a sneer about it.

It reminded Maigret of somebody, but who it was, he couldn't tell.

"Jusqu'à mon jour dernier."

Anna's was a grave voice, almost masculine. Slowly it faded away. Then:

"Do you want me to go on, *Monsieur le commissaire?"*

He quickly shut the doors of the cupboard, slipped the photograph into his pocket, and noiselessly darted back into Joseph's room, before answering:

"No. That'll do, thank you."

He noticed that Anna was paler when she came upstairs. Had she perhaps put a little too much feeling into the song? She looked round the room, but could find nothing unusual.

"I don't understand. . . . But never mind. . . .

I wanted to ask you something, Inspector. You saw Joseph last night. What do you think of him?"

She had removed the kerchief from her head, and Maigret even fancied she had washed her hands.

"We must," she went on, "we absolutely must establish his innocence. It must be recognized by everybody. . . . We've got to make him happy. . . ."

"With Marguerite Van de Weert?"

Anna merely sighed.

"How old is your sister Maria?"

"Twenty-eight. . . Nobody doubts that she'll one day be headmistress of her school at Namur."

Maigret felt the photograph in his pocket.

"Has she ever had any love-affairs?"

The answer was spontaneous:

"Maria?"

The tone made the meaning clear.

"Maria have a love-affair? . . . Little do you know her!"

"I'll be getting on with my work," said Maigret, going out onto the landing.

"Have you found out anything yet?"

"I don't know."

She followed him downstairs. In the kitchen he saw the old man, who had just taken his place in the wicker chair, and who appeared not even to see them as they passed.

"He doesn't notice anything nowadays," sighed Anna.

There were three or four people in the shop.

Madame Peeters was filling glasses with gin. She bowed slightly to Maigret, without relinquishing the bottle or interrupting the conversation she was holding in Flemish.

She was probably telling them that this was the great inspector who'd come all the way from Paris, for everyone turned towards him and their looks were full of respect.

Outside, Machère was examining a bit of ground where the soil seemed looser than elsewhere.

"Found anything?" asked the inspector.

"I'm afraid not. I'm still looking for the body. For unless we find it, we shall never get these people."

He looked at the Meuse in a way which seemed to indicate that at any rate the body had not gone that way.

4
A Picnic from the Past

IT was a little after twelve. For the fourth time that morning, Maigret was walking along the river-bank. On the other shore was a long stretch of whitewashed wall, belonging to the factory. Through the gateway dozens of workers, men and women, were pouring out and wending their way homeward, on foot or cycling, to their mid-day meal.

Maigret was about a hundred yards from the bridge when the stream of factory-hands began to pass him. One face caught his attention instantly. He turned round to look again, only to find the other had turned too.

It was the person whose photograph he had in his pocket.

A moment's hesitation, then the young man stepped up to the inspector.

"Are you the detective from Paris?"

"You're Gérard Piedbœuf, aren't you?"

The detective from Paris! He was getting used to the phrase, and he knew by now exactly what it meant. Machère had been sent over from Nancy to take charge of the case. He was there by right, and anyone who had any information to give went straight to him to give it.

Maigret, on the other hand, was "the detective from Paris," an interloper who had been called in by the Belgians for the sole purpose of whitewashing them. And whenever he was recognized in the street, the glances that were turned on him were anything but friendly.

"Are you coming from our house?"

"No. But I was there this morning earlier. I missed your father, however. He'd already turned in."

Gérard was no longer quite so young as in the photograph. He was still very young both in face and figure, and in the way he dressed, but, looking closely at him, you could see he was on the wrong side of twenty-five.

"Did you want to see me?" he asked.

Whatever his faults were, shyness was not one of them. His eyes looked steadily into Maigret's. Brilliant, dark brown eyes, eyes which would certainly win favor with women, particularly with his olive complexion and well-drawn mouth.

"Oh! I've hardly got down to work yet. . . ."

"On behalf of the Peeters; I know. Everybody knows. In fact, it was known all over the town before you ever set foot in the place. They say you're a friend of the family and are making it your business to prove . . ."

"To prove nothing at all! . . . Ah! There's your father getting up."

They could see the little house. On the first floor a blind was pulled up and a man with a heavy gray mustache was just visible looking out of the window.

"He's seen us," said Gérard. "He'll soon be dressed."

"Do you know the Peeters personally?"

They started walking up and down the quay, from one bollard to the next, about a hundred yards from the Flemish shop. The air was keen. Gérard's overcoat was too thin, but as he obviously liked the cut of it, he probably didn't mind.

"What do you mean?"

"For three years or more your sister was Joseph Peeters' mistress. Was she received in his house?"

The other shrugged his shoulders.

"Have we got to go through the whole story in detail? . . . First of all—that is, just before the child was born—Joseph swore he'd marry her. . . . Then Dr. Van de Weert came and offered my sister ten thousand francs to clear right out and never come back. . . . The first time Germaine went out after having the baby was to take it round to the Peeters to show it them. They made a frightful scene, and the old woman called her all the names she could think of. . . . After that, things got a bit better. And Joseph was all the time promising to marry her. . . . Only, he kept on saying that he must pass his exams first. . . ."

"And you?"

"Me?"

At first he pretended not to understand. Then all at once he changed his tune. The smile that came to his lips was both conceited and sarcastic as he went on:

"Has anybody told you anything?"

Without pausing in his stride, Maigret took the photograph from his pocket and showed it to his companion.

"Heavens! I'd never have thought that was still in existence!"

He raised his hand to take it, but the inspector put it back in his pocket.

"Did she give it you? . . . No. It's impossible. She's too proud. . . . Unless . . . Now . . ."

During the conversation Maigret never took his eyes off Gérard. Was he tuberculous, like his sister? It was hard to say. But he certainly had the kind of attractiveness that so often goes with consumption—finely chiseled features, good complexion—with lips that were sensual and slightly derisive.

He was well dressed in a cheap way. Without waiting for the body to be found, he had put a crêpe armlet on his beige overcoat.

"Did you make love to her?"

"It's an old story. It happened long ago—before Germaine had the kid. It must be at least four years ago. . . ."

"Go on. . . ."

"There's my father on the doorstep taking a breath of fresh air."

"Go on, all the same."

"It was on a Sunday. . . . The Peeters were taking Germaine to the Rochefort Caves. But at the last moment one of the sisters dropped out and I was asked to make up the party. . . . They're about fifteen miles away. . . . We had a picnic. We laughed a lot. I was in very good form. . . . Then, after lunch, we paired off. Joseph and Germaine, Anna and me. We wandered about in the woods."

Maigret's eye still rested heavily on him, but it expressed nothing.

"And then?"

"And then! . . . Yes. . . ."

A silly and rather unpleasant smile spread over Gérard's face.

"I really couldn't tell you just how it happened. I don't waste much time when it comes to that sort of thing, and she was taken unawares."

Maigret put a hand on the young man's shoulder, and spoke the words slowly:

"Is that true?"

Yes, it was true. Maigret was convinced of it. Anna would have been twenty-two at the time.

"And then?"

"Nothing more. Look at her! What would you

expect me to do with a girl like that? . . . In the train she stared at me the whole time, and it was obvious that the less I had to do with her the better."

"What did she do about it?"

"Nothing. I avoided her, and she must have understood. For if ever I ran into her in the street her eyes were like a pair of revolvers."

They were approaching the Piedbœufs' house now. Gérard's father, in his carpet slippers, came a few steps to meet them.

"I hear you called this morning. . . . Won't you come in? Have you told the inspector all about it, Gérard?"

Maigret went into the passage. The staircase looked as though it was made of matchwood. Everything was poor and ugly. The kitchen was the only sitting-room. Its table was covered with oil-cloth with a large blue pattern.

"Who killed her?" asked Piedbœuf, whose intelligence was evidently of a low grade. "She went off, saying she'd had no news of Joseph for weeks and that he was a month behindhand. . . ."

"A month behindhand?"

"Yes. He's been paying a hundred francs a month all along on account of the child. He couldn't do less, could he? You see, it's like this . . ."

Fearing his father was going to embark on a long rigmarole, Gérard quickly intervened.

"The inspector isn't interested in all that. What he wants are facts. And there's one fact that can't be got away from, and that is, that Joseph Peeters was here on the evening of the 3rd, however much he may swear he wasn't."

"You're referring to the man who says he saw his motor-bike? I'm afraid that's not much good now. Another fellow passed this way a little after eight that evening, and he was riding a motor-bike of the same make."

"Ah!"

And more aggressively:

"Just what we thought! You're on their side."

"I'm not on anybody's side. I'm merely trying to find out what happened."

But Gérard only sneered. Turning to his father, he went on:

"The inspector's only come here to see if he can trip us up."

And then to Maigret:

"You'll excuse me, won't you? Lunch is ready, and I have to be back in the office by two."

What was the good of arguing? Maigret cast a final look round him, caught sight of a child's cot in the next room, then walked along the passage and let himself out.

*

Machère was waiting for him at the *Hôtel de la Meuse*. The commercial travelers were having lunch in a small room, separated from the café by a partition with a glass-paneled door. But meals were also served, for those who preferred it, on the marble tables of the café itself, and there were a few people eating as Maigret entered.

Machère was not alone. Sitting at the same table, with an *apéritif* before him, was a short man with a monstrously long mustache and arms as long as a hunchback's. Both men stood up as Maigret approached.

"The skipper of the *Etoile Polaire,* Gustave Cassin," announced Machère, whose eyes shone brightly.

Maigret sat down. A glance at the saucers that had accumulated in two little piles told him they had had three drinks apiece.

"Cassin has something to tell you."

Indeed he had! He was bursting with it. With an air of great importance he leant over towards the inspector.

"Say what you've got to say—that's right, isn't it? Only, no need to say it till you're asked to. That's what my father used to say. No need to go butting in."

"Un demi!" called out Maigret, ordering a glass of beer.

He pushed his bowler onto the back of his head and unbuttoned his overcoat. Then, while the bargee was groping for his words, he cut in:

"If my information's correct, on the night of the 3rd you were drunk as a lord."

"Not as drunk as all that. Not by any means. I'd had two or three glasses, but I could walk straight. And what's more, I could see straight."

"Did you see a motor-bike draw up at the Flemish shop?"

"Me? . . . Certainly not."

Machère made a sign to Maigret not to interrupt the man, to whom he nodded encouragingly.

"I saw a woman on the quay. . . . And I can tell you which one it was. The one who never serves in the shop and who takes the train every day. . . ."

"Maria?"

"She might be called Maria, but I don't know anything about that. But I know it was the thin one, with fair hair. . . . And now tell me this: is it natural she should be wandering about on the quay in a wind sharp enough to go right through you?"

"What time was it?"

"The time I was going back to bed. It might have been eight o'clock; it might have been later."

"Did she see you?"

"No. For instead of going straight on as I was going, I slipped behind the customs house and watched. I thought it could only be a man as could bring a girl out on a night like that, and I thought I might see a bit of fun."

"You've been had up, I hear, for assaulting girls."

Cassin grinned, showing a horrible set of rotten teeth. He might have been any age. His face was heavily lined, but the hair, which grew low on his forehead, was not yet turning gray.

He was eager to know the effect he was producing. After each sentence he looked at Maigret, then at Machère, then at a man sitting at the next table, who was listening to the conversation.

"Go on."

"She wasn't looking for a man. . . . She was looking to see there was *nobody!*"

Cassin paused to let the words sink in. He swallowed down his drink in one mouthful and called out to the waiter:

"The same again."

Then out it came:

"She was looking to see the coast was clear. And then some other people came out of the house—by the back door. And they were carrying something long. Long and heavy it was. And they threw it into the Meuse, just between my boat and the *Deux Frères,* which was the next one downstream."

"Waiter! The bill, please."

Maigret didn't seem in the least astonished. Machère was disconcerted, and so was the bargee.

"Come along with me."

"Where?"

"Never mind. Come."

"But I'm waiting for the drink I ordered."

Maigret waited patiently till it was brought and duly swallowed. Then, telling the landlord he'd be back for lunch a few minutes later, he took the old drunkard out onto the quay.

The latter was deserted at that time of the day, everybody having returned home for lunch. Big drops of rain began to fall. Machère had followed them out.

"Now! Show me exactly where you stood."

He was already familiar with the customs

house. He watched Cassin take station in a corner.

"And you didn't budge from there?"

"I should think not. I didn't want to get mixed up in anything."

"Come out of it!"

And Maigret went and stood in his place.

He didn't stay there many seconds. Then, looking straight at Cassin, he said:

"You'll have to think of something better than that, my friend."

"What do you mean?"

"I mean what I say. In other words: it won't wash. . . . From that corner you can't see the shop at all, nor the part of the river you spoke of."

"When I said I was there, I meant. . . ."

"That'll do! I tell you, you've got to think up something better than that. When you have, you can come and see me again! And if it doesn't hold water . . . Well! There's a very good chance of your being locked up again."

Machère was crestfallen. He in turn took up his position in the corner. What Maigret had said was incontestable.

"You're quite right," he groaned.

As for the bargee, he didn't say another word. With lowered head, he stared at Maigret's feet, and his eyes were venomous.

"Don't forget what I've told you. If your next story isn't more plausible than that, we'll clap you in jail. . . . Come along, Machère. . . ."

And Maigret turned on his heel and made for the bridge, filling his pipe as he went.

"Do you think Cassin . . . ?"

"I think it won't be very long before he's back again with another story to incriminate the Peeters."

"All the same . . . We have to listen to evidence. If he's got any . . ."

"He certainly will have!"

"What evidence?"

"How should I know? . . . But he'll think of something."

"To clear himself?"

But Maigret changed the subject by asking for some matches, having used all his own trying vainly to light his pipe in the wind.

"I'm sorry. I haven't any. I don't smoke."

Machère wasn't sure what Maigret said next, but it sounded rather like:

"I ought to have known it!"

5
At the "Café de la Mairie"

THE rain had started at lunch-time. It had increased before dark, and by eight o'clock had turned into a downpour.

The streets of Givet were empty. The barges glistened with wet. Maigret, with his coat collar turned up, trudged along towards the Flemish shop, pushed open the door, ringing the now familiar bell, and plunged into the warm atmosphere of coffee and spices.

It was at that time of the day on the 3rd of January that Germaine Piedbœuf had entered the shop, never to be seen by her family again.

Maigret hadn't noticed before that the door to the kitchen was paneled with glass. A muslin curtain was drawn across it, so that he could hardly make out the people on the other side.

Someone got up.

"All right! It's only me."

And he walked straight through into the kitchen, thrusting himself abruptly into the private life of the family. It was Madame Peeters who had risen to go and serve in the shop. Her husband was in his wicker chair, as usual, so close to the stove that he looked in danger of catching fire. He was holding a clay pipe with a long stem of wild cherry, but he wasn't smoking. His eyes were shut and his mouth half-open, and his breathing came regularly.

As for Anna, she was sitting at the deal table, scrubbed with silver sand and polished with the years. She was totting up figures in a little account-book.

"Take the inspector into the sitting-room, Anna."

"Please don't move," answered Maigret. "I've only looked in for a moment."

"Well, take your coat off, anyhow."

Another thing the inspector noticed for the first time was that Madame Peeters had a beautiful voice. It was low, grave, and caressing, and the Flemish accent made it all the more attractive.

"And you'll have some coffee, won't you?"

He wondered what Madame Peeters had been doing before his arrival, but the question was no sooner formulated than it was answered by the evening paper lying on the table and the steel-rimmed glasses that had been hastily put down.

He had butted in on a typically homely scene. The old man's breathing seemed like the pulse of this quiet house. Anna shut up her account-book and fetched a cup and saucer from the dresser.

"I was hoping to see your sister."

Madame Peeters shook her head sadly, while Anna explained:

"I'm afraid you won't be seeing her for some days. That is, unless you go to Namur. One of the mistresses, who also lives at Givet, called a little while ago to tell us that Maria was laid up. When she got out of the train this morning, she slipped and sprained her ankle."

"Where is she?"

"At the convent. They've put her up."

Still shaking her head, Madame Peeters sighed:

"I don't know what we've done for God to send us all this trouble."

"And Joseph?"

"He won't be back again till Saturday. . . . But I was forgetting—that's tomorrow."

"Have you seen any more of Marguerite?"

"Only in church. At Vespers."

Steaming coffee was poured into his cup. Madame Peeters disappeared for a moment, returning with a wine-glass and a bottle of gin.

"It's old Schiedam schnapps."

Maigret sat down. He wasn't expecting to find out anything. In fact, his presence there was not wholly a matter of duty.

The house reminded him of Holland. His thoughts ran back to the case which had taken him to Delfzijl. Certainly there were differences. But here was the same calm, the same density of the air, the same feeling that the atmosphere was not fluid, but was composed of some solid substance that would be shattered if you moved.

Now and again the old man's chair creaked, though he never moved. With his patient, even breathing he seemed not so much to be living as marking time.

Anna said something in Flemish, the meaning of which Maigret guessed as:

"You ought to have brought a bigger glass."

From time to time a man in sabots would pass along the quay. The rain could be heard pattering on the shop window.

"I think you said it was raining on the 3rd? Was it raining as hard as it is now?"

"Yes. I think so."

The two women had resumed their seats. They watched Maigret raise his glass to his lips. In fact, Anna's eyes never left him.

Her features was not so delicate as her mother's. Nor did she possess her mother's benevolent, indulgent smile. Had she missed the photograph he had pinched from her room? Probably not. Surely her face would have betrayed it.

"It's thirty-five years since we came here," said Madame Peeters. "We started off with just the wicker business. Then we added the shop, and then we built another story on the house."

But Maigret's mind was wandering. He was picturing Anna four years younger, walking in the woods with Gérard Piedbœuf.

How had it happened? What sudden streak

of wildness had assailed her? Or was Gérard really the expert hand he made himself out to be? What had she thought about it afterwards?

One thing Maigret felt pretty sure of. It was the one and only adventure of her life, and would always remain so.

There was something overpowering about the atmosphere of this house. Partly as a result of the schnapps, a dull warm glow gradually pervaded his brain. All the same, his senses were acutely alive. Not a sound escaped him—a little squeak from the wicker chair, a gentle snore from the old man, the slightest increase or decrease in the pattering rain. . . .

"Would you like to play me that piece again?" he asked Anna. "The one you played this morning."

She was on the point of protesting, but her mother chimed in:

"Yes. Do. . . . She plays well, doesn't she? She had three lessons a week for six years from the best teacher in Givet."

Anna went into the sitting-room, leaving the two doors open behind her. They could hear her opening the piano, then her right hand running casually over the keys.

"She ought to sing," murmured Madame Peeters. "Though, of course, Marguerite has a better voice. There was even a question of her taking it up properly and going to the conservatoire."

The notes swelled in the quiet house. Anna had started playing. The old man still slept unheeding, and his wife, fearing he might drop his pipe, took it gently from his hand and hung it on a nail in the wall.

What was Maigret doing there? Was he working? Was he following some clue?

Madame Peeters listened, glancing frequently at her paper, which she would have liked to go on with. Another person ought to have been sitting at that table—Maria correcting her pupils' exercises.

And that was all.

Or would have been, if all the town hadn't been accusing them of a ghastly murder, committed on just such an evening as this.

Maigret started at the sound of the shop bell. For a second, he could almost have fancied that he was three weeks younger and that this was Germaine Piedbœuf come to claim her little monthly allowance of a hundred francs.

It was a bargee in oilskins, who produced a little bottle for Madame Peeters to fill with gin.

"Eight francs."

"In Belgian money?"

"No. In French. Or ten Belgian francs if you'd rather."

Maigret got up and crossed the shop.

"Are you going already?"

"I'll be looking in again tomorrow."

Outside he saw the bargee making towards his boat. The inspector turned round to look at the house. With its shop window lit up, it looked like a stage setting, largely because of the music, faintly audible behind the scenes.

Gentle, sentimental music. Anna was singing now:

"Mais tu me reviendras,
O mon beau fiancé."

Maigret splashed through the puddles. The drenching rain soon put his pipe out.

And now it was the whole of Givet which looked like a stage setting. The bargee had disappeared, and he was thus the only person left on the stage. All round him, nothing but the subdued lights showing through curtained windows, and the roar of the rushing Meuse, which gradually obliterated the music.

When he had gone some two hundred yards or so, he had both houses in sight. Behind him, the Flemish shop; on the right, close to, the Piedbœufs' cottage.

There was no light upstairs, but the passage was lit up. The child would be in bed now. Would anybody else be in the house? Not much fun for a young man like Gérard, sitting there all alone. Or perhaps the midwife . . .

Maigret was fed up. Rarely had he had such a feeling of the futility of what he was about.

Indeed, what was he about? He hadn't been sent there. The Peeters were accused of murdering a girl, but there was nothing whatever to show she was even dead.

Perhaps she'd had as much as she could stand of her dismal life in Givet. Perhaps she'd cleared out. Perhaps she was at that moment in Brussels, Rheims, or Paris, having a drink with friends she'd picked up.

Even if she was dead, it didn't necessarily mean she'd been killed. What sort of a reception had the Peeters given her? Had they made her despair of ever marrying Joseph? And had she gone straight out and thrown herself into the river?

No proof. Not even a decent clue. Wasn't Machère doing all he could? Yet he wasn't getting anywhere, and it looked as though the case would in the end simply be pigeon-holed unsolved.

Why should Maigret have allowed himself to become involved in it? Once more: what was he doing there? There was no doubt of the answer most people in Givet would have given to that question! He had been hired by the Belgians to whitewash them!

Just opposite him, on the other bank of the river, was the factory, whose yard was lit up by a single electric lamp. The only other light came from the night-watchman's lodge at the gate.

Old Piedbœuf would be on duty now. What would he do with himself to pass the night away?

And without exactly knowing why, Maigret, with his hands deep in his overcoat pockets, made straight for the bridge. In the bar he'd been in that morning, the bargees and tug skippers were talking so loudly that their words carried right across the quay, but he didn't stop.

The wind made the girders of the steel bridge vibrate. It had been built to replace the old stone

one destroyed during the war. On the other side, the quay wasn't even paved, and Maigret had to plow his way through the mud. A stray dog was sheltering close in under the whitewashed wall.

As Maigret approached the gate, Piedbœuf's face appeared at the door of the lodge.

"Good evening," said Maigret.

The man was wearing an old military tunic dyed black. He was smoking a pipe. In the middle of the room was a small round stove, whose stove-pipe, after a couple of elbows, went out through the wall.

"You know, it's not allowed . . ."

"To come in here at night. Never mind! It's all right," and the inspector went in.

A wooden bench. A cane-seated chair. Maigret's overcoat began to steam.

"Do you spend the whole night in here?"

"Except when I'm going the rounds. That's three times during the watch."

At a distance, his mustache was rather imposing, but close to, he was far from being impressive. A timid man, one might almost say shrinking, dominated by an abiding sense of his own lowly station.

He was ill at ease in Maigret's presence, and did not know what to say to him.

"So you spend most of your life alone. . . . At night, here. The mornings in bed. . . . What do you do with your afternoons?"

"Gardening."

"I didn't know you had a garden."

"I do the midwife's. We share the vegetables."

Maigret noticed some mounds in the cinders. Investigating with a poker, he discovered potatoes in their skins.

He could picture the man in the middle of the night, eating his baked potatoes as he stared vacantly into space.

"Does your son ever come to keep you company?"

"Never."

An irregular trickle of raindrops dripped down from the roof outside the door.

"Do you really think your daughter was killed?"

Piedbœuf did not answer at once. His eyes flitted restlessly from one object to another.

"If Gérard says so. . . ."

And all at once, with a sob in his throat:

"She'd never have killed herself. . . . And she'd never have gone off. . . ."

A sudden note of tragedy that had been quite unexpected. The old man knocked out his pipe and refilled it, but his thoughts seemed far away.

"Do you know Joseph Peeters well?"

Piedbœuf turned his head away.

"Well enough to know he'd never marry her. There's money in that family . . . while we . . ."

On the wall was a beautiful electric clock, the only luxurious thing in the little shelter. On the opposite wall was a blackboard on which had been chalked: *No men wanted.*

"It's time I was going the rounds."

Maigret nearly offered to come with him, not that he particularly wanted to see the factory, but he would have liked to know more of the old watchman. The latter put on a loose oilskin, which reached down to his heels, and picked up a storm-lantern which was already burning, so that all he had to do was to turn up the wick.

"What I don't understand is why you should be against us . . . though I suppose it's natural enough. . . . Gérard says . . ."

But they were outside now, and the conversation was put a stop to by the rain and the wind. Piedbœuf accompanied his visitor to the gate. Looking through it, Maigret had a fresh vision of Givet, a vision divided into vertical strips by the iron bars. The barges lying alongside the other bank of the river; the Flemish shop with its window still lit up; the quay with its lamps every fifty yards, each with a halo of light made by the rain; the town beyond. . . .

The customs houses stood out quite clearly, and it was easy to make out the corner of the little side-street whose second house on the left was the Piedbœufs'.

The 3rd of January.

"Has your wife been dead long?"

"It'll be twelve years next month. It was chest trouble that took her."

"What would Gérard be doing at this time of the evening?"

The lantern swung slightly at the end of the watchman's arm. He had already put a large key in the lock of the little side-gate, which he had to lock up before going his rounds. A train whistled in the distance.

"He'll be knocking around somewhere in the town."

"I suppose you don't know where?"

"The young people mostly get together at the *Café de la Mairie*."

And Maigret trudged off again through the darkness and the mud. This didn't seem like a case at all. There was really nothing to go on. Nothing whatever.

It was only a handful of people that he had to do with in this little wind-swept town. Each of them went about his business in the usual way. Perhaps all of them were perfectly sincere in what they told him.

One of them, on the other hand, was perhaps a tortured soul suffering an agony of dread at the thought of Maigret's massive figure prowling about the streets that night.

He came to his hotel, but did not go in. Through the window, he could see Machère holding forth to a group of men who were doubtless at their fourth or fifth round. The landlord was amongst them—in fact, he was apparently standing another round at that moment.

Machère was gesticulating. He was obviously in good form. He was probably saying:

"These inspectors who come from Paris haven't the faintest idea. . . ."

And of course they were talking of the Belgians, tearing them to ribbons.

At the end of a narrow street was a fairly spacious square. In one corner, a white-painted café with three windows brightly lit up. It was the *Café de la Mairie*.

The door opened onto a hum of conversation. A bar covered with zinc. Marble-topped tables, on some of which were the usual little squares of red baize for the card-players. The air thick with pipe and cigarette-smoke and a sour smell of beer.

"Deux demis, deux!"

Orders were shouted out to the waiter, who hurried backwards and forwards in his white apron.

Sitting down at the first table he came to, Maigret immediately caught sight of Gérard Piedbœuf in one of the misty mirrors on the wall. He too, like Machère, was holding forth, but he stopped abruptly at the sight of the inspector, nudging his companions, who all looked in the latter's direction.

There were three at the table besides him. A young man and two girls, the latter no doubt factory-girls.

All round, the buzz of conversation died down. Even the card-players made their calls in subdued voices, while glances from all sides were turned on the newcomer.

"Un demi, un," ordered Maigret.

And Gérard Piedbœuf, with a scornful smile on his face, muttered half-audibly:

"The Belgians' friend. . . ."

He had been drinking, certainly. His eyes were too brilliant. His purple lips exaggerated the pallor of his complexion. He was obviously excited, and was in the mood to play to the gallery. He groped for something appropriate to say.

"You know, Ninie, one day, when you're a rich woman, you'll have nothing to be afraid of—particularly from the police."

His neighbor kicked him under the table, to make him shut up, but the result was only to spur him on.

"What are you kicking me for? . . . Isn't this a free country? Can't you say what you think? . . . I'm not afraid to speak my mind anyhow, and I tell you that if you've got money the police will eat out of your hand, but if you haven't . . ."

But he hadn't quite as much nerve as he pretended. He looked a bit white about the gills. Really he was scared by his own audacity, but the desire to show off was stronger.

Maigret flicked away the foam which covered his beer and took a deep draught. The silence would have been absolute if it hadn't been for the card-players.

"High tierce!"

"Four knaves!"

"Your deal!"

"Cut, will you?"

And the two little factory-girls, who didn't dare turn towards the inspector, shifted in their seats so as to be able to watch him in the glass.

"It seems to be a crime in France to be a Frenchman—particularly if you're poor. . . ."

The proprietor, sitting at the cash-desk, frowned and threw appealing glances at Maigret, as though begging him to understand that the young man was drunk. But Maigret didn't even notice him.

"Et pique! . . . Et encore pique," said a card-player triumphantly. "You weren't expecting that, were you?"

"People who've made a fortune out of smuggling," went on Gérard, taking care everybody could hear him. "There's not a person in Givet that doesn't know it. . . . It used to be cigars and lace. And now that spirits are forbidden in Belgium they can do a roaring trade in gin with the bargees. . . . It's not difficult, that way, to make your son a lawyer. . . . Just as well for him he is a lawyer. He'll need all the tricks of the trade when they put him in the dock."

Maigret sat all by himself at his table, the focus of all eyes. He hadn't taken off his overcoat, and the raindrops glistened on his shoulders.

It certainly looked as though it would end in a scuffle, and the proprietor came up to the inspector in an attempt to smooth things over.

"I hope you won't take any notice. He's been drinking. . . . And the loss of his sister . . ."

"Come on, Gérard! Let's go," said one of the factory-girls anxiously.

"What for? Do you think I'm afraid?"

Gérard's back was turned towards Maigret, and they could only see each other by means of the mirrors.

The card-players were only playing half-heartedly, making mistakes, and forgetting to score.

"Some brandy!" ordered Gérard. "Liqueur brandy. . . ."

The proprietor was on the point of refusing, but he didn't want to precipitate a scene. He looked inquiringly towards Maigret, but the latter made no sign.

"A dirty, filthy, rotten business! . . . First of all they take our girls, and then cut their throats when they've had enough of them. . . . And the police . . ."

But Maigret was picturing the night-watchman going round the workshops in his uniform tunic, dyed black, with his storm-lantern to light him on his way. How long would it take for those potatoes to cook?

His mind wandered back to the town side of the river. The Piedbœufs' house. The child sleeping in its railed-in cot. The midwife knitting or reading the paper, waiting till Gérard came home.

Further off, the Flemish shop. They'd have wakened the old man and taken him upstairs to bed. Madame Peeters pulling down the shutters. Anna all alone, undressing in her room.

And the barges sleeping in the Meuse, bumping each other, straining at their hawsers, their rudders creaking, the water swirling under their keels.

"Waiter! Another *demi!*"

Maigret's voice was calm. He smoked away slowly at his pipe, blowing little puffs towards the ceiling.

"Just look at him! Sitting there sneering. . . ."

The proprietor was at his wit's end. There was obviously going to be a row, and he felt impotent to stop it.

For Gérard had risen as he spoke and was now facing Maigret. His features were drawn, his lips twisted with anger.

"I tell you, that's all you came to Givet for—just to make fools of us all. Look at him! Sneering away! . . . All because I've had a glass or two . . . or rather, because I haven't as much money as some people. . . ."

"Hearts!" declared a card-player, trying to create a diversion.

But he was punished for his pains, for Gérard snatched the cards out of his hand and sent them flying across the room.

Half the customers were on their feet by now. They did not know what to do, but held themselves ready to intervene as soon as the sparks began to fly.

But Maigret remained quietly in his place, puffing slowly at his pipe.

"Look at him, I tell you! He's sneering at the lot of us. He knows perfectly well my sister's been murdered."

The proprietor hovered nervously about. The two little factory-girls exchanged anxious glances and their eyes measured the distance to the door.

"He doesn't dare open his mouth! What could he say if he did? He'd only make the truth stick out the plainer."

"I assure you he's drunk," pleaded the proprietor piteously, seeing Maigret at last rise from his chair.

But nothing could stop it now. Poor Gérard! He was more scared than anybody, as Maigret's somber and ponderous mass advanced towards him.

Gérard's right hand dived swiftly into a pocket, and at the same moment a woman screamed.

For what emerged from the pocket was a revolver. It didn't remain long, however, in Gérard's hand. A lightning grab from Maigret, a swift movement of his foot, and the young man tripped and went sprawling on the floor.

Everybody was standing now. Yet not one person in three realized what had happened. All they could see now was a revolver in the inspector's hand and Gérard on the floor.

And while Maigret slipped the revolver in his pocket as simply and naturally as if it had been his tobacco-pouch, the young man snarled:

"You're going to arrest me, I suppose?"

He had risen no further than on to his hands and knees. He cut a truly pitiful figure.

"Run along," said Maigret quietly, "and go to bed."

And, as Gérard didn't appear to understand, he added:

"Open the door, someone!"

A blast of cool air blew into the suffocating atmosphere. Holding him by the shoulder, Maigret pushed Gérard out into the street.

"Run along. . . ."

The door closed. There was one person the less in the café: Gérard Piedbœuf.

"He'll sleep it off," muttered Maigret, returning to his table and sitting down in front of his glass of beer.

There was an awkward silence. Some people were sitting down again. Others hesitated.

Maigret drank a mouthful of beer, then sighed:

"Never mind! It's all in the day's work!"

Then, turning to one of the card-players, he added:

"I think you said hearts were trumps. . . ."

The man didn't know quite what to answer, seeing that his cards still lay scattered on the floor!

6
The Hammer

MAIGRET had decided to take it easy the following morning. It wasn't really laziness, but rather that he didn't know what to do with himself. Ten o'clock had just struck when he was wakened in a disagreeable manner.

First of all there was a violent knocking on his door, a thing he detested at the best of times. And then, as he slowly came to his senses, the first thing that greeted them was the patter of rain on the balcony.

"Who is it?"

"Machère."

The name came through the door like a triumphal trumpet-blast.

"Come in!"

And then:

"Draw back the curtains, will you?"

Maigret lay in bed, while the room was suddenly flooded by the raw light of a thoroughly nasty day. Beneath his window a fishwife was trying to palm off her wares on the landlord of the hotel.

"I've some news for you. It came by the first post."

"Just a moment. Would you mind shouting down the stairs and telling them to send up my breakfast? The bell doesn't work."

Maigret reached for his pipe that lay ready filled within reach.

"News of what?"

"Of Germaine Piedbœuf."

"Dead?"

"Dead as mutton."

Machère said it with the utmost satisfaction, at the same time drawing from his pocket a four-page letter on foolscap, adorned with all manner of official stamps.

It had been passed on from one authority to another. Machère ran through the headings:

"Transmis par le Parquet de Huy au Ministère de l'Intérieur à Bruxelles.

"Transmis par le Ministère de l'Intérieur à la Sûreté Générale à Paris.

"Transmis par la Sûreté Générale à la Brigade Mobile de Nancy.

"Transmis à . . ."

"Cut it short, will you, old man?"

"Very well. What it boils down to is this . . . the body was fished out of the Meuse at Huy—that's about seventy or seventy-five miles from here. It was found five days ago. . . . Of course

I'd had a notice sent out to all police stations along the river, but they'd forgotten about it and . . ."

"Can I come in?"

It was the maid with the coffee and the *croissants*. As soon as she had gone, Machère started off again.

"But I'd better read it to you. . . . *This twenty-sixth day of January, one thousand nine hundred and . . .*"

"No, old chap! For Heaven's sake come to the point."

"Well, it seems practically certain that she was murdered. It's no longer a moral certainty, but a material one. Listen to this:

"The body, as far as can be judged, has been in the water about ten days or a fortnight. Its state of . . ."

"Oh, come on!" groaned Maigret with his mouth full.

". . . *decomposition* . . ."

"Yes. I know. But let's come to the conclusions and skip the description."

"There's a whole page of it."

"Of what?"

"Description . . . Very well, then—if you don't want to hear it. . . . They seem a little doubtful on some points. But one thing is quite certain: Germaine Piedbœuf was dead for a considerable time before being immersed in water. The medical report says: *two to three days*. . . ."

Maigret was dipping his *croissant* into his coffee and munching pensively, while staring out of the window. In fact, Machère broke off, thinking he was no longer listening.

"Of course . . . if this doesn't interest you . . ."

"Go on!"

"There's a detailed account of the post-mortem. Would you like to hear it? No? Then we come straight to the most interesting part. The skull was found to be bashed in in one place, and the doctors say it was done by some blunt instrument, like a hammer, and that in all probability this was the cause of death."

Maigret thrust one leg out of the bed, then the other. He stared at himself in the glass for a moment before starting to lather his face. While he shaved, Machère went on reading from the typewritten document in his hands.

"Don't you think it's extraordinary? . . . I don't mean about the hammer, but the fact that the body was only thrown into the water two or three days after the crime. I shall have to go and have another look over the house."

"Do they give a list of the clothing found on the body?"

"Yes. . . . One moment. . . . Here it is. . . . *Black shoes with a strap across the instep, soles and heels fairly worn. Black stockings. Pink underclothes of poor quality. Black serge dress (no maker's name).*"

"Is that all? . . . No overcoat?"

"No. . . . That's funny."

"It was the 3rd of January, cold and raining."

Machère's face clouded.

"Admittedly . . ."

"Admittedly what?"

"She wasn't on such friendly terms with the Peeters that she'd be invited to take off her coat. . . . On the other hand, if they'd removed it, why didn't they strip her completely, so as to make identification harder?"

Maigret washed so vigorously that he even splashed Machère in the middle of the room.

"Do the Piedbœufs know?"

"Not yet. I thought perhaps you'd like to . . ."

"To do nothing of the sort! Don't forget I'm not here officially. You carry on just as if I'd never come."

He hunted for his collar-stud, and at last finished dressing.

"I must be off now," he said, pushing Machère out of the door. "I'll see you again later."

*

He walked along aimlessly. He had come out just to be out of doors, or, more precisely, to plunge once more into the atmosphere of the town, and he didn't care where his legs carried him. It was just a matter of luck that he suddenly found himself staring at a brass plate on which was engraved:

Docteur VAN DE WEERT
Consultations de dix heures à midi

A few minutes later, in spite of the three patients who sat waiting their turn, he was ushered into the presence of a little man, whose complexion was childishly pink, and whose hair was as beautifully white as Madame Peeters'.

"I'm glad to see you, Inspector. But I hope it's nothing disagreeable. . . ."

He rubbed his hands together as he spoke. A buoyant optimism radiated from his whole person.

"My daughter told me about you. It's very kind of you to . . ."

"I'd like first of all to ask you a question: Does it require much force to smash a woman's skull with a hammer?"

The little man's consternation was a sight to see. He wore a morning-coat of a cut that had long been out of fashion. A massive watch-chain was stretched across his stomach.

"A woman's skull? . . . How should I know? At Givet, I've never had occasion to consider such a question."

"Do you think, for instance, that a woman would be strong enough?"

It was altogether too much for the doctor, who gesticulated excitedly.

"A woman? . . . My dear sir! . . . You're surely not suggesting that a woman would think of . . . ?"

"Are you a widower, Dr. Van de Weert?"

"I have been for twenty years. Fortunately my daughter . . ."

"What do you think of Joseph Peeters?"

"What could I think? He's an excellent fellow. . . . I would certainly have preferred him to take up medicine, as he could have taken over my practice. . . . But there you are. He seems to be gifted for law. And it's a fine profession."

"What about his health?"

"Quite all right. Of course he's been working very hard, and he may be a bit run down. And then being so tall. . . . He shot up a bit too quickly, perhaps. . . ."

"There's no taint in the Peeters family?"

"A taint?"

He pronounced the word with such alarm that one might have thought he'd never heard of hereditary diseases.

"Really, Inspector! Your questions take me rather by surprise. You've seen my cousin, Madame Peeters. If you ask me, she'll live to a hundred."

"And your daughter?"

"She's more delicate. She takes after her mother. . . . May I offer you a cigar?"

A real Flemish type. He could have stepped straight out of a picture or an advertisement for some brand of schnapps. Full, bright red lips, and clear blue eyes that revealed all the simplicity of his soul.

"And Mademoiselle Marguerite was due to marry Joseph?"

The doctor's face clouded ever so slightly.

"Yes. We were expecting them to marry one day or another. If it hadn't been for this . . . this unfortunate . . ."

He couldn't find the right word for it. But for him it was just something unfortunate.

"Strange, isn't it?" he went on. "They couldn't see how much better it would be for everybody for the girl to accept a little pension for herself and the child, and if possible to go and live in some other town. . . . As a matter of fact, I think it was her brother who was at the bottom of it all."

Maigret hadn't the heart to condemn him. He was so obviously sincere, so obviously well-meaning. His very innocence blinded him to all the harsher realities of life.

"To say nothing of the fact that the child was never proved to be Joseph's. . . . If we'd found a good home for her and the child . . ."

"So your daughter was waiting till it had all blown over?"

Van de Weert smiled.

"She's been in love with him from the age of fourteen. Beautiful, isn't it? . . . And it wasn't for me to raise objections. . . . Have you got a match? . . . If you want my candid opinion, there hasn't been any crime at all. That girl has always been running after men, and now she's suddenly gone off with one. And her brother's making the most of her disappearance, hoping to make a good thing out of it. . . ."

It didn't occur to him to ask Maigret's opinion. He was quite convinced his version was the right one. He pricked his ears as sounds reached them from the waiting-room. No doubt the patients were getting restive.

And with an eye as innocent as the doctor's, the inspector calmly asked his final question:

"Do you think Mademoiselle Marguerite is Joseph's mistress?"

Van de Weert came very near to being indignant. The blood mounted to his forehead. But the feeling that gained the upper hand was one of sadness that anyone could be so uncomprehending.

"Marguerite? . . . Are you mad? . . . Who could ever have invented such a thing? . . . That Marguerite should be the . . . the . . ."

Maigret's hand was already on the handle of the door, and without so much as a smile he took his leave and went out. In the house was a mixed smell of cooking and pharmaceutics. The maid who hastened to open the front door was as fresh as if she'd just stepped out of a hot bath.

Outside, he was once more in the rain and the mud. Passing lorries splashed the pedestrians.

It was Saturday. Joseph Peeters was due that afternoon, and he'd be staying till the following evening. In the *Café des Mariniers* a lively discussion was going on, for news had just come through from the *Ponts-et-Chaussées* that the river was now open to navigation from the frontier right down to Maestricht.

Only, on account of the strength of the current, the tugs were asking fifteen francs a ton per kilometer instead of ten.

They were also eagerly discussing a barge loaded with stones which had broken away from its moorings and fallen foul of the bridge at Namur and sunk, obstructing one of the arches.

"Any casualties?" asked Maigret.

"The bargee was ashore, but his wife and son were drowned. He was having a drink when they hauled him out of the bar. He ran down to the quay, but it was too late to do anything, as she was already out in the stream. . . ."

Gérard Piedbœuf passed on his way home to lunch. This time he was cycling. A minute or two later, Machère appeared, coming back from the Flemish shop, where he had no doubt broken the news. Turning the corner, he went and rang the Piedbœufs' door bell. The door was opened by the midwife, who received him coldly.

*

"So you've been had up for assaulting girls? . . . Tell me all about it."

On board most barges, the living-quarters are kept in a state of cleanliness rarely equaled in private houses. But that was not the case with the *Etoile Polaire*.

Gustave Cassin was unmarried, and what little domestic work was done, was done by a lad of twenty who was epileptic and not quite all there.

The cabin smelt rather like a barracks. Cassin was busy on a hunk of bread and cold sausage, which he was washing down with a bottle of red wine.

More sober than usual, he looked guardedly at Maigret and was some little time making up his mind to speak.

"It wasn't really an assault at all. I'd already been to bed with the girl two or three times. . . . One evening I met her on my way and she refused to have anything to do with me, saying that I was drunk. All I did was to catch hold of her wrist, but she yelled out as though I was murdering her. Some *gendarmes* happened to be passing, and as luck would have it I caught one of them on the chin with my fist and bowled him clean over."

"Did you get five years?"

"I thought I was going to. The little bitch swore she'd never had anything to do with me. Fortunately I had some witnesses, though the judge didn't seem to believe all they said, but it helped me out a lot. In fact, I'd have got off with a year if it hadn't been for the *gendarme,* who was in hospital for a fortnight. . . ."

He cut off a bit of bread with his sailor's knife.

"Would you like a drink? . . . We may be off tomorrow. . . . But I want to know more about this lighter that's obstructing the bridge at Namur. . . ."

"And now tell me why you invented that story about the woman standing on the quay."

"What story?" asked Cassin, trying to gain time.

"Come on! Admit that you never saw anything at all."

Maigret did not fail to observe the flicker of glee that came into the bargee's eye.

"Do you think so? Well, perhaps you're right."

"Who asked you to do it?"

"Who asked me?"

The little flame still danced in his eye. He spat out a bit of sausage-skin without even bothering to turn his head.

"Where did you come across Gérard Piedbœuf?"

"Ah, I wonder!"

The two men were as placid the one as the other.

"Did he give you anything?"

"He stood me a few drinks."

Then, suddenly changing his tone, he went on, with a chuckle:

"Only, it isn't true. I was only saying it to please you. . . . And if you'd like me to say the same to a judge and jury, you've only to say the word."

"What did you see, really?"

"If I told you, you wouldn't believe me."

"Go on, all the same."

"All right. . . . I saw a woman waiting. Then a man came and she threw herself into his arms."

"Who were they?"

"How could I tell, in the dark?"

"Where were you?"

"Coming back from a *bistro*."

"Where did the couple go? To the Flemish shop?"

"No, they went behind."
"Behind what?"
"Behind the house. . . . On the other hand, if you'd rather that it wasn't true . . . You see, I know the ropes. There were any amount of lies told at my trial, and my lawyer told more than anyone."
"Do you go sometimes to have a drink in the Flemish shop?"
"Never. They refuse to serve me. All because I brought my fist down once, and they say I broke their scales. They want people to stand there and get drunk without ever moving or saying a word."
"Did Gérard Piedbœuf talk to you?"
"What did I tell you just now?"
"That he'd asked you to say . . ."
"Would you really like to know the truth? . . . Well, here it is, and this time it's God's own truth, and that is, that I can't stand the sight of a policeman, and you no more than any other. You can repeat that to the magistrate, and I'll swear you beat me up, and what's more, I'll show the marks. . . . Not but what I wouldn't give you a glass of red if you've a mind for one."
Maigret looked hard into his eyes, then suddenly stood up.
"Show me round," he said curtly.
Was he surprised? Was he alarmed? Or merely disagreeable? Whichever it was, Cassin, with his mouth full, made a face.
"What is it you want to see?" he growled.
"Just a moment!"

Maigret went up on deck, returning a moment later with a customs officer whose oilskin shone with rain.

"I've already been cleared by the customs," said Cassin scornfully.

Maigret turned to the officer.

"I suppose all the bargees do a certain amount of smuggling?"

"Except that I wouldn't call it 'a certain amount'!"

"Where do they generally hide the stuff?"

"At one time they had a way of keeping it in watertight cases right under their boats. But nowadays we run a chain under the hull to make sure there's nothing there. . . . Then there's the space between the cabin flooring and the bottom. For that we drill a few holes in the flooring with that huge brace you may have seen on the quay."

"Anywhere else?"

"What's your cargo?" asked the officer.

"Scrap iron," answered Cassin.

"That's awkward. . . ."

Maigret's eyes never left Gustave Cassin, hoping he'd give himself away by an instinctive glance towards a hiding-place. But the man went on eating ostentatiously, sitting obstinately in his chair.

"Stand up."

The order was obeyed, but with obvious reluctance.

"So I haven't the right to sit down in my own cabin!"

On the chair was a filthy cushion, which Maigret promptly seized. Three sides of it were neatly sewn, but the fourth was done with big clumsy stitches, which betrayed an unpracticed hand.

"Thank you, that's all," said Maigret to the customs officer.

"You think there's some contraband here?"

"No. I don't think so after all. Many thanks."

The customs officer regretfully left them. As soon as he was gone, Maigret asked:

"What have we here?"

"Nothing."

"Do you generally keep such hard objects in your cushions?"

He ripped open the seam, disclosing something dark inside. A moment later he was unfolding a small coat, creased and crumpled, made of black serge.

There was no doubt in the inspector's mind that it was the same serge as that of the dress described in the report which Machère had read to him that morning. Like the dress, the coat had no maker's name. Germaine Piedbœuf had made them both herself.

But it wasn't the coat that was the most interesting thing. Unrolling it, Maigret had come to a hammer, whose shaft was smooth with long use.

"The funny thing about it," muttered Cassin, "is that it's going to lead you right up a blind alley! . . . I haven't done a thing. Nothing, that is, except pull those two things out of the Meuse on the 4th of January early in the morning."

"And you thought you'd like to keep them to yourself?"

"It's a habit of mine," answered Cassin, with an air of self-satisfaction. "Are you going to arrest me?"

"Is that all you have to say?"

"Yes. Except that you're going to be led right up the alley."

"And you'll soon be sailing?"

"Not if I'm arrested!"

To the man's astonishment, Maigret carefully stuffed the things back in the cushion, slipped it under his overcoat, and went ashore without another word.

Cassin watched the inspector walking along the quay past the customs officer, who saluted respectfully, then he went below again, scratched his head, and poured himself out another drink.

7
A Jacket on the Quay

RETURNING to his hotel for lunch, Maigret was told that the postman had brought a registered letter for him, but had refused to leave it in his absence.

That meant he'd have to go to the post office to fetch it. Not a very serious matter. But it was one of a series of incidents that were calculated to try his temper.

During lunch he enquired after Machère. No one had seen him, and a telephone call put through to his hotel elicited the fact that he had left half an hour before. Maigret had, of course, no right whatever to give orders to the local police, but he had wanted, all the same, to give Machère the tip to keep an eye on Gustave Cassin.

At two he was at the post office, where they handed him his letter. A stupid business. Some furniture he had bought, but had then refused to pay for, as they hadn't sent the things he'd ordered. And now the dealer was threatening to sue him.

It took a good half-hour to compose an answer, and then he had to write to his wife about it, telling her just what to do.

Before he had finished he was rung up by the director of the *Police Judiciaire,* who enquired how long he was staying, and asked him a number of questions about some other cases that were in hand.

Out of doors it was still raining. He was sitting in the *salle de café* of his hotel, the floor of which was strewn with sawdust. There was no one else there except the waiter, who was taking advantage of a quiet moment to do some writing himself.

It was only an absurd little fad, but Maigret loathed writing on marble-topped tables.

"Ring up the *Hôtel de la Gare* again, will you? Ask if the detective's back yet."

Maigret was in a vague state of ill-humor, which was perhaps all the worse for having no serious reason. Two or three times he got up and stared out through the misty window. The sky was a shade brighter, and the rain less heavy, but the quay was still deserted.

About four o'clock, the inspector heard a blast on a steam-whistle. He ran to the door and saw a puff of steam rising from a tug. It was the first sign of any activity since his arrival.

The stream was still running swiftly. The tug

shoved off from the quay, and she seemed literally to stagger as the current caught her. She looked so thin and slight, a thoroughbred in comparison to the hulking great barges, and for a moment it looked as though she would be swept headlong down the river. But she held her own, stemmed the tide.

Another blast, longer and more strident. A hawser tautened at her stern, and one of the barges detached itself from the others. The tug was turning now, towing the barge's nose out into the stream. In the barge, two men were leaning with all their weight against the tiller.

At the entrances of the other cafés, customers had gathered to watch. Two other barges were under way now, and then the last towing-line tautened and a fourth was dragged out into the stream. By this time, the tug was far down the river, whistling proudly, while her four tenders swept out a half-circle across the river, then lined up behind her as best they could.

The *Etoile Polaire* was not one of them.

*

. . . and I beg you to take the first opportunity of sending for the furniture which was sent in error.

Maigret read through his first letter carefully. Then, taking an envelope, he wrote out the address. He wrote abnormally slowly, as though his fingers were too big for his pen, and he pressed his nib hard down on the paper. The letters themselves were small, but all the lines, up-strokes as well as downstrokes, were fat.

"There's Monsieur Peeters on his motor-bike," said the waiter, who had switched on the lights and was now drawing the curtains.

It was half-past four.

"He must be in love with it to do a hundred and twenty-five miles on a day like this. He's covered with mud from head to foot."

"Albert! . . . Telephone!"—the landlord's wife called out.

Maigret stuck up his envelope and stamped it.

"It's for *Monsieur le commissaire,*" said Albert, returning from the telephone. "A call from Paris."

Maigret spoke with the over-gentle voice of a man who's trying not to lose his temper. His wife was at the other end, enquiring when he'd be back.

"And they've been bothering again about that furniture."

"I know. It's all right. I've just been seeing to it."

"Then there's a letter from your opposite number in England. . . ."

"*Oui, ma chérie*. It's not important."

"Is it cold up there? Wrap up well, won't you? I'm sure you haven't got rid of that cold, and . . ."

Why should he be a prey to such impatience? It was so acute, it was hurting him. Yet it was only a vague impression, an impression something was going on and he was missing it.

"I ought to be back in three or four days."

"Not before?"

"It's hardly likely. . . . Good-by. I must be off now. . . ."

Back in the café, he asked where the mail-box was.

"At the corner, at the tobacconist's."

It was nearly dark, and little could be seen of the river except the reflected lights of the other bank. The inspector could just make out a figure leaning against a tree. It at once struck him as odd, for, what with the cold and the rain, it was hardly the weather for loafing about in the open.

He slipped his letters into the box, then turned back. As he did so, the figure detached itself from the trunk of the tree and followed.

It was done in a trice; Maigret turned swiftly on his heel, took four or five quick strides and had the fellow by the collar.

"What are you doing here?"

The man went red in the face from Maigret's stranglehold.

"Answer, will you?"

There was something disconcerting about the man, something about his evasive eye which made you uncomfortable; and his smile was still worse.

"Aren't you the chap who works aboard the *Etoile Polaire?*"

The other nodded, looking thoroughly pleased at being recognized.

"And you were watching me, weren't you?"

Maigret remembered what he had been told: that the fellow was an epileptic and mentally deficient. On his face was an odd mixture of happiness and fear.

"Don't grin! Tell me what you were doing."

"Watching you."

It was impossible to be severe with the wretch, who was all the more pitiful for being in the years of ripening manhood. Twenty!

He didn't shave, yet it was only a few thin fair hairs that were scattered over his chin. His mouth seemed twice as big as it ought to be.

"Don't hit me. . . ."

"Come along."

Some of the barges had shifted berth. For the first time for weeks there was an air of activity about them. One or two women were coming ashore to do their shopping. Customs officers were going from boat to boat.

The barges that had proceeded that afternoon had left the *Etoile Polaire* lying alone. There was a light in the cabin.

"You go first."

The barge was separated from the quay by several feet of water, and the only way to go on board was over a gangway that consisted of a single and all too flexible plank. In spite of the light in the cabin, there was no one on board.

"Where does your skipper keep his Sunday clothes?"

It wasn't lost on Maigret that the disorder was worse than usual. The lad opened a cupboard and gaped. In a heap at the bottom were Cassin's everyday clothes.

"And his money?"

A vigorous shaking of the head. The half-wit didn't know. Perhaps Cassin took care he didn't.

"All right. You stay here."

Maigret walked off pensively, staring at the ground. Almost bumping into a customs officer, he asked:

"Have you seen Cassin of the *Etoile Polaire?*"

"No. Isn't he on board? He's supposed to be sailing first thing tomorrow morning."

"Does the barge belong to him?"

"Good gracious, no! But it's in the family. It belongs to a cousin of his who lives at Flémalle, a creature as daft as himself."

"How much money would he be likely to earn?"

"Cassin? Perhaps something like six hundred francs a month. . . . A bit more with the smuggling, but even then not very much."

The house on the frontier was lit up. Not only the shop, but upstairs too.

A minute or two later the shop bell rang, and Madame Peeters could be heard bustling across the kitchen. And Maigret, wiping his feet on the mat, called out:

"It's only me."

*

The only person in the sitting-room was Marguerite Van de Weert, who was turning over the pages of some music.

She looked fluffier than ever in a pale blue satin dress as she gave the visitor a welcoming smile.

"You've come to see Joseph?"

"Isn't he here?"

"He's upstairs, changing. . . . He's mad to come by road in weather like this. And he ought to be looking after himself—he's overworked as it is. . . ."

It wasn't love—it was adoration! You could hear it in her voice. You could tell at once that she was capable of sitting hours at a time gazing at him.

What was there about him that inspired such feelings? And his sisters seemed to share them too.

"Is Anna with him?"

"She'll be hanging his wet clothes up to dry."

"Have you been here long?"

"About an hour."

"You knew Joseph would be coming?"

The faintest cloud passed over her features, but was gone almost as soon as it had come.

"He comes every Saturday. And it's always about this time."

"Is there a telephone in the house?"

"Not here. We have one at home, of course. A doctor can't do without one."

He didn't know why, but Maigret was beginning to dislike her. To be more exact, she was getting on his nerves. She affected rather babyish ways, and her eyes were meant to be so very candid.

"Here he is. He's coming downstairs."

There were steps on the stairs, and a moment later Joseph Peeters came in, clean and tidy, his hair slicked down, with the comb-marks still showing.

"I didn't know you were here, Inspector."

He wasn't sure whether he ought to shake hands or not, and before he had decided, the moment had slipped by. Turning to Marguerite, he said:

"Have you asked the inspector to have a drink?"

A number of people were speaking Flemish in the shop. Anna came into the room with her usual quiet, self-possessed air, bowing as she had no doubt been taught to bow in some convent school.

"Is it true that there was some trouble last night in the *Café de la Mairie?* We heard something, but you know how people exaggerate. . . . But do sit down—Joseph, fetch something to drink, will you? . . ."

Maigret was trying to formulate a vague impression that he had had immediately on entering the room. More than once he was on the point of putting his finger on it, but each time he missed it.

Something was changed, but for the life of him he couldn't tell what it was.

The result was to plunge him into one of his sulking moods. His face was shut and forbidding. What he really wanted was to do something eccentric, or even outrageous, just to break the spell.

As for Anna, she was more of a mystery to him than ever. He knew less and less what to think of her. She was wearing the same gray dress she had worn all along, a dress which somehow made her seem imperishable as a statue.

Had external events any hold over her? Whatever happened, she seemed untouched. Her movements were grave, calculated, competent. Her face was serene.

She might have been a character that had stepped out of Greek tragedy, bringing her antique gestures with her, to move about in the humdrum little world of this house astride the frontier.

"Do you ever serve in the shop?"

He used the word *magasin* for shop. He was going to use the humbler word *boutique*, but corrected himself in time.

"Yes, often. Whenever my mother's busy. . . ."

"You serve drinks too?"

She didn't smile. She simply raised her eyebrows.

"Why ever not?"

"I suppose the bargees get drunk sometimes? Do they ever try to take liberties?"

"Never in our place!"

That was just like her. Sure of herself. Firm as a statue.

"Would you like some port, or . . . ?"

"If I may, I'd rather have some of the old Schiedam schnapps you gave me yesterday."

"Go and ask *Maman* for a bottle of 'old.' "

Joseph obediently disappeared.

Which made it look as though Maigret had

miscalculated in estimating the status of the various members of the family. In his list Joseph had come first, as veritable lord and master of the family. Then Anna. Then Maria. Then Madame Peeters, whose duty it was to mind the shop. Last of all, the old father sleeping in the wicker chair.

But however much they might adore Joseph, it appeared to be Anna, not he, who gave orders.

"Have you discovered anything fresh, Inspector? . . . You saw that the barges were leaving, didn't you? . . . They say the river's open down to Liége, possibly even to Maestricht. In a couple of days we'll have no more than three or four here at a time."

Why was she telling him that?

"No, Marguerite! The stemmed wine-glasses. . . ."

Marguerite was taking some small tumblers from the sideboard.

Maigret was still itching to say or do something that would disturb the equilibrium, and now that Joseph was out of the room and Marguerite busy with the glasses, he took the opportunity of showing Anna the photograph of Gérard Piedbœuf.

"I want to speak to you about it," he whispered.

He watched her closely. But if he had expected to disturb her serenity, he was disappointed. She merely made a little sign, a sign of understanding, a sign which meant:

"Yes, yes. But later on. . . ."

And to her brother, who came back into the room, she said:

"Are there still a lot of people in the shop?"

"Five."

Anna was by no means blind to the subtleties of life. The bottle Joseph had brought was fitted with a thin metal spout which enabled the contents to be poured out quickly without a drop being lost.

Before pouring out the schnapps she removed the appliance, which served much too commercial a purpose to be permitted in the parlor.

Maigret warmed his glass for a moment in the hollow of his hand. Then he raised it to Joseph, who was the only one to drink with him. Joseph raised his glass in turn.

"It's now been proved that Germaine Piedbœuf was murdered."

Marguerite was the only one to make a sound. She uttered a little ladylike scream such as is used on the stage. And then:

"How awful!"

"Machère said something of the sort, but I wasn't going to believe him," said Anna. "I suppose that will make our position still more difficult."

"Or possibly easier. Particularly if I'm able to prove that your brother was not in Givet on the 3rd."

"Why?"

"Because Germaine Piedbœuf was killed by heavy hammer-blows."

"Good God! . . . You can't mean it! . . ."

It was Marguerite who spoke, standing rigid, deathly pale, all ready to faint.

"I've got the hammer in my pocket."

"No, no! . . . Please! . . . Don't show it!"

Anna, however, remained calm. Turning to her brother, she said:

"Has your friend returned?"

"Yesterday."

"It's another student," Anna explained to the inspector, "the one he spent the evening with —the evening of the 3rd. They were together in a café in Nancy. . . . But ten days ago he was called to Marseilles on account of his mother's death. Now he's back. . . ."

"A votre santé," answered Maigret, emptying his glass.

Then he took the bottle and filled it up again. From time to time the shop bell rang, or there would be the sound of sugar being shoveled into a paper bag, or the clink of coins.

"How's your sister?"

"She may be up on Monday or Tuesday, but we're not expecting her here for some little time."

"Is she engaged?"

"Oh, no! She wants to be a nun. It's an idea she's been nursing for a long time."

Maigret sensed that something was going on in the shop. The sounds were the same, but the voices a trifle subdued. Had the shop bell rung? He couldn't be sure. But a moment later Madame Peeters was saying in French:

"You'll find them in the sitting-room."

Steps crossed the kitchen, and there was

Machère, standing in the doorway, obviously very excited, but making a great effort to keep calm. He looked at the inspector sitting at the table with his glass of schnapps in front of him.

"What is it, Machère?"

"It's . . . Well . . . I'd like to have a word with you. . . ."

"What about?"

"About the . . ."

He broke off, making signs to Maigret that were obvious to everybody.

"Don't be shy."

"It's about the bargee . . . Cassin. . . ."

"He's come back?"

"No . . . He . . ."

"He's confessed to something?"

Machère was on the rack. He had come to discuss a matter which he considered of the utmost importance. A confidential matter too, and he was being made to blurt it out in front of a roomful of people.

"He . . . His cap's been found, and his jacket."

"Which ones? The old or the new?"

"I don't understand."

"Was it his Sunday clothes? Cloth or serge?"

"Dark blue cloth. The jacket was lying on the quay."

Everyone was silent. Anna, who was standing, looked fairly and squarely at the young detective without moving a muscle. Joseph's hands were fidgeting nervously.

"Go on."

"He must have thrown himself into the Meuse.

His cap was found in the water. It was carried downstream, but got caught by one of the fenders of the next barge."

"And the jacket?"

"Was lying on the quay with a note pinned to it."

He took the note cautiously from his wallet. A shapeless scrap of paper that had been soaked with rain, the words barely legible.

"I'm a rotter. The river's the best place for me."

Maigret read it out half-audibly. In an anxious voice, Joseph asked:

"I don't understand. What does it mean?"

Marguerite looked from one face to the other, with her big expressionless eyes. Machère was still standing in the doorway. He was ill at ease.

"I think it was you . . ." he began, addressing Maigret, "you who . . ."

Maigret stood up. His sulky look had completely disappeared, giving way to a genial cordiality. When he spoke, his words were addressed chiefly to Anna.

"There you are! . . . I was telling you about a hammer, wasn't I?"

"Please!" Marguerite pleaded.

"What are you doing tomorrow afternoon?"

"The same as any other Sunday. We generally stay at home together. We shall miss Maria. . . ."

"If you allow me, I'd like to call on you. Perhaps you'll be making one of your excellent *tartes au riz. . . .*"

With that, Maigret went out into the passage and put on his overcoat, which the rain had made twice as heavy as usual.

"If you'll excuse me . . ." muttered Machère.

"Yes. You come along with me."

In the shop, Madame Peeters was standing on a little stepladder, fishing for a packet of starch on one of the highest shelves. A bargee's wife was waiting mournfully at the counter, her shopping-basket hanging from her arm.

8
A Visit to the Ursulines

A SMALL group of people had gathered at the place where the jacket had been found. But Maigret did not stop. Dragging Machère with him, he walked straight on towards the bridge.

"You hadn't said anything to me about the hammer, so I suppose . . ."

"What have you been doing all day?"

Machère looked rather like a guilty schoolboy.

"I went to Namur. . . . I wanted to make sure that Maria Peeters really had sprained her ankle."

"Well?"

"They wouldn't let me in. The nuns looked at me as though I was a savage."

"Did you insist?"

"Indeed I did. I even threatened them."

Maigret suppressed a smile. Going into a gafrage by the bridge, he asked for a car to take him to Namur. It was thirty miles by the road which ran along the banks of the Meuse.

"Are you coming with me?"

"Do you want me? . . . But I tell you, they won't let you in. Besides, now that we've found the hammer . . ."

"All right. There's another job you could do. Hire a car yourself and go to every little station within a radius of ten or fifteen miles. Make sure Cassin hasn't made off by train."

Maigret drove off. Snuggling well down into the back seat, he smoked serenely, seeing nothing of the landscape but the lights which flicked past intermittently on either hand.

He knew that Maria Peeters was a *régente* in a school kept by the Ursulines. And he knew that the latter held in the teaching world a position comparable with that of the Jesuits, with whom they formed, so to speak, the aristocracy of Catholic education. Their school in Namur would doubtless be frequented by all the swagger families of the Province.

And Maigret was decidedly tickled by the thought of young Machère trying to force his way in, and even resorting to threats.

"I forgot to ask him what he'd called them," thought Maigret with a chuckle. "Probably *mesdames*. . . . Or perhaps *ma bonne sœur*. . . ."

Maigret was tall, broad-shouldered, massive and heavy-featured, but when he rang the convent bell in a little street where grass grew between the cobble-stones, the lay sister who opened the door was not in the least alarmed.

"Might I speak to the Reverend Mother?"

"She's in the chapel. But as soon as Benediction is over . . ."

And he was shown into a waiting-room, in comparison with which the Peeters' sitting-room was all dirt and squalor. Here, looking at the floor was little short of looking in a mirror. But what was more impressive even than the cleanliness was the feeling that every object had stood in the same place from time immemorial, that the clock on the mantelpiece had never stopped, nor ever been a minute fast or slow.

From the sumptuously tiled corridors came the sound of gliding footfalls and occasional whispers, and from further off the faint sound of an organ.

The people of the Quai des Orfèvres would doubtless have been astonished to see their Maigret very much at ease. When the Mother Superior arrived he bowed with due discretion, and when he began speaking he addressed her in the proper fashion:

"*Ma mère* . . ."

She waited, her clasped hands hidden within her voluminous sleeves.

"I must apologize for troubling you, but I would like your permission to visit one of your teachers. Of course I know it's against the rules, but the life of somebody is at stake—or at any rate the liberty—I thought perhaps . . ."

"Are you from the police too?"

"Yes. I believe you've already had a visit from a detective."

"A gentleman who said he belonged to the police. He made rather a disturbance, and went off shouting that we'd hear more about it before long."

Maigret apologized for the incident. He spoke quietly, politely, deferentially, and after a few well-chosen phrases a lay sister was sent to warn Maria Peeters that she would be receiving a visitor.

"I believe you think very highly of her, *ma mère?*"

"Very highly indeed. We hesitated to take her at first on account of her parents' business. It wasn't their being shopkeepers, but the fact that they served drinks. In the end we waived the objection, and we've never regretted it for a moment. . . . Recently she arrived limping, having sprained her ankle getting out of the train, and we put her to bed. . . . She's very upset about it, as she hates giving trouble to others. . . ."

The lay sister returned. Maigret followed her along interminable corridors. On the way, he passed several groups of pupils, all of them dressed alike: pleated black smocks, a blue silk ribbon round the neck.

At last they came to a door on the second floor, and the lay sister, having opened it, asked whether she should stay or not.

"Perhaps you'd better leave us, *ma sœur*."

A little room of austere simplicity, the walls painted with oil-paint and hung with religious lithographs in black frames, and a large crucifix.

An iron bedstead. A thin figure hardly perceptible beneath the bed-clothes.

No face was visible, nor did the invalid speak. The door was shut behind him, and Maigret stood waiting, looking distinctly out of place in his thick wet overcoat and his bowler in his hand.

At last he heard a stifled sob. But Maria Peeters still kept her face turned to the wall and covered as much as possible by the bed-clothes.

"Calm yourself," he murmured. "Your sister, Anna, must have told you to look on me as a friend."

But, far from calming her, he seemed only to make her worse. Her whole body was shaken by sobs.

"What does the doctor say about it? . . . Will you be laid up for long?"

It's embarrassing to have to talk to an invisible person. Still more if it's a person you've never even seen.

But the sobbing gradually subsided. Maria was making an effort to get herself under control. She sniffed, and her hand groped for a handkerchief under the pillow.

"What is it that's upsetting you? . . . The Reverend Mother has been telling me how much they appreciate you here."

"Leave me alone," she pleaded.

At the same moment there was a knock on the door, and the Mother Superior entered as though she had sensed that it was the right moment to intervene.

"I hope you don't mind, but I know how sensitive poor Maria is."

"Has she always been like that?"

"She has a rather delicate nature. . . . And as soon as she realized she would be laid up for some days, and that someone else would have to take her classes, she had a bad attack of nerves. . . . Let us see your face, Maria."

A vigorous head-shaking from the girl in bed.

"Of course we know all about the trouble in the family, and the cruel things that are being said. I've had three masses said for the truth to come to light. And I've just been praying for you at Benediction, Maria."

At last the latter showed her face. A miserable little face, all pinched and pale, except for the red blotches that came from crying.

She was not in the least like Anna. She had her mother's delicacy of line, only her features were so irregular that she could not possibly have passed for pretty. The nose was too long, too pointed, the mouth long and thin.

"I'm sorry," she said, dabbing her eyes with her handkerchief. "I'm too easily upset, I know. But the thought of being in bed here while others . . . You're Inspector Maigret, I suppose? . . . Have you seen my brother?"

"I left him a little more than an hour ago. He was at home with Anna and your cousin Marguerite."

"How is he?"

"He's all right. He seems quite confident."

Was she going to start crying again? The Reverend Mother looked encouragingly at Maigret. She liked the calm authority with which he spoke, and felt it was bound to reassure the patient.

"Anna told me you were thinking of taking the veil. . . ."

The tears flowed afresh. Maria had no thought for her looks, and did not attempt to hide her shiny blotchy face.

"We've been expecting it for a long time," said the Mother Superior. "Maria belongs to us much more than to the world."

The thought of it threw Maria into another fit of sobbing. Her chest heaved, her legs twitched, and she clutched the bed-clothes convulsively.

"You see how right we were to refuse to let the other gentleman see her."

Maigret was still standing in the middle of the room, looking positively enormous in his heavy overcoat. He looked at the little bed, and the wretched sobbing girl.

"Has a doctor been?"

"Yes. He says the sprain's nothing. The real trouble is the nervous disturbance it has given rise to. . . . Perhaps we'd better leave her now—that is, if you've finished. . . . Come, now! Calm yourself, Maria. I'll send Mère Julienne in to stay by you for a bit."

The image he took away with him was that of a white bed, hair sprawling over the pillow, and an eye fixed on him as he backed out of the room.

In the corridor the Mother Superior spoke in subdued tones as she glided along the polished floor.

"She's never been very strong, and this unhappy scandal has thoroughly unnerved her. Her fall itself was no doubt due to nerves. . . . She's ashamed of the trouble her brother's got into, and more than once she's said that of course we couldn't receive her into our Order now. She's had terrible moods of despondency, gazing at the ceiling for hours at a time and refusing to take her food. . . . Then suddenly it'll take her the other way, and she'll be shaken to pieces by sobs. . . . She's been given injections. . . ."

They had reached the ground floor.

"Would you mind if I asked you what you thought about the case, Inspector?"

"Not at all. But I should be very much at a loss for an answer. . . . Honestly, I don't know what to think. . . . Tomorrow, perhaps . . ."

"Tomorrow?"

"And now I have only to thank you, and to apologize for having troubled you, *ma mère*. I might perhaps take the liberty of telephoning to ask after the patient."

At last he was outside, breathing the chill air, saturated with moisture. He found his car drawn up by the curb.

"Back to Givet."

Once more he nestled down into the upholstery of the car and blissfully filled his pipe. At some cross-roads near Dinant he caught sight of a sign-post!

Grottes de Rochefort. . . .

It flashed past too quickly for him to read the number of kilometers, but he caught a glimpse of a road that led away into the darkness. It set him thinking, thinking of a fine Sunday, a train packed with excursionists, two couples: Joseph Peeters and Germaine Piedbœuf—then Anna and Gérard.

A hot sunny day. And no doubt the excursionists, on their homeward journey, carried armfuls of flowers.

Anna, sitting in the train, battered yet thrilled by what had happened, furtively eyeing the man who had changed the meaning of her life.

And Gérard, thoroughly pleased with himself, talking and showing off, with no thought of the gravity of what was for him merely a lark.

Was it broken off then and there? Or did either try to renew it?

"No," answered Maigret to himself. "Anna must have understood. Before nightfall she must have had no illusions left, and from that day she must have avoided him."

And he pictured her guarding her secret, fearing for months the possible sequel to that afternoon, hating Gérard, stiffening, holding up her head, and setting her face against all romance.

"Shall I take you to your hotel?"

They were at Givet already. The Belgian frontier with its khaki-clad customs officer, then the French frontier, the quay, the barges.

Maigret was quite surprised to feel the heavy object he had in his overcoat pocket. He had forgotten all about it.

Machère had heard the car arrive, and when Maigret had paid off the driver, he found the young detective standing at the entrance of the *Café de la Meuse*.

"Did they let you in?"

"Of course."

"Not really? I felt sure they wouldn't. As a matter of fact, I thought they had a very good reason. I thought she wasn't there at all."

"Where else would she be?"

"I don't know. It's getting beyond me. Particularly since that hammer was discovered. . . . Do you know who's been to see me?"

"Gustave Cassin?"

They were in the café now, and Maigret, choosing a corner seat near the window, ordered a *demi*.

"Not Cassin. . . . That is, not quite. But it comes to much the same thing. I'd been round to all the stations without any result. Then Gérard Piedbœuf came to look me up."

"To tell you where the man was hiding?"

"To say that Cassin had been seen getting into the 4.15 at the station here in Givet. It's the Brussels train."

"Who saw him?"

"A friend of Gérard's. He said he'd bring him along if I wanted to see him."

"Dinner for two?" asked the landlord.

"No. . . . Yes. . . . Just as you like. . . ."

Maigret took a long, greedy draught of beer, then asked:

"Is that all?"

"I should have thought it was quite enough! . . . If he was really seen at the station, it means he isn't dead. And what's more, it means he's running away. . . . If that's the case . . ."

"Naturally."

"You think the same as I do?"

"I don't think anything at all, Machère. I'm hot one moment and cold the next. In other words, I think I'm in for a real streaming cold. In fact, I think bed's the best place for me. . . . Waiter! Another *demi!* No. Make it a hot grog. With plenty of rum. . . ."

"Has she really sprained her ankle?"

Maigret didn't answer. He had suddenly fallen into a somber mood. He even looked anxious.

"I suppose the examining magistrate has given you a blank warrant?"

"Yes, but he told me to be very careful how I used it. It's so easy to stir up trouble in a little town. If possible, he wants me to ring him up before taking any drastic steps."

"And what are you thinking of doing?"

"I've already wired to the *Sûreté* at Brussels to ask them to arrest Cassin as he steps off the train. I must ask you to give me the hammer."

To his neighbor's astonishment, the inspector produced a hammer from his pocket and laid it on the marble table.

"Is that all you want?"

"You'll have to make a statement, since it's you who found it."

"Oh, no! No need to say it's me. Officially, you found it yourself."

Machère's eyes shone with joy.

"Thanks. That's very good of you. Things like that count for promotion."

"I've laid two places near the stove," said the landlord.

"Thank you. But I'm going to bed. I couldn't face a meal."

And Maigret shook his companion by the hand, and went up to his room.

He had had a cold hanging about him for days, and trudging about in wet clothes had certainly made it no better. He went to bed feeling worn out. For half an hour he tossed about, with unformed images playing havoc with his mind, but finally he went off into a heavy sleep.

The next morning, however, he was little the worse for wear. No one else was up when he came down, except the waiter, whom he found in the café lighting the percolator, then putting ground coffee into the upper part.

The town was still sleeping. Darkness was only now giving place to daylight, and the lights were still burning. The only sign of life outside was on the river. Voices could be heard calling from barge to barge. Towing-lines were passed through fairways and turned up round bollards. A tug slowly approached, taking up station at the head of the line.

Another convoy was off to Belgium and Holland.

It wasn't actually raining, but the finest of drizzles was enough to wet your shoulders as you walked through it.

Some church bells started ringing. A light went on in one of the windows of the Flemish shop. Then the door opened, to be carefully closed again by Madame Peeters, who then hurried off with a cloth-bound missal in her hand.

As soon as she returned, she opened up the shop, then went and lit the kitchen fire.

It was nine o'clock before Joseph appeared on the doorstep—and even then he was unshaven, uncombed, and without a collar.

At ten he reappeared in hat and coat and went to church with Anna. The latter wore a new coat of beige cloth.

Maigret was out all the morning, wandering about, except when he went from time to time into a café to warm himself with a glass of spirits. The people who knew were saying it was going to freeze, which would be a catastrophe for the flooded regions.

At the *Café de la Mairie* were a number of bargees waiting for news of a tug which was expected at any moment. They were waiting to know whether the skipper would be prepared to sail again the same day with the barges that were in a hurry to be off. Now and again one of them would rise from his seat and go out to stare downstream.

It was almost twelve when Gérard Piedbœuf left home, in his Sunday best: brown shoes, a light gray hat, gloves. Passing close to Maigret, his first idea was to ignore him.

But he couldn't. He was itching to get his own back.

"I hope I'm not in your way," he sneered. "Of course I know you can't stand the sight of me. . . ."

His eyes were sunken. Since the little row in the *Café de la Mairie* his nerves had been perpetually on the stretch.

Maigret shrugged his shoulders and turned his back. He watched the midwife put the child in a pram and wheel it off towards the center of town.

No sign of Machère. It wasn't till one o'clock that Maigret came across him. It was in the *Café de la Mairie,* and Gérard was there too, with the same people he had been with on Friday night.

Machère was at a table with three other men, and Maigret had the feeling he had seen them before. He was duly introduced.

One was the deputy mayor, and one of the other two his secretary. All of them were in their best clothes and were drinking some kind of aniseed *apéritif*. It was by no means their first: in fact, there was a pile of three saucers at each plate. Machère's self-assurance was a trifle exaggerated.

"I was just telling these gentlemen that the case is practically finished. . . . It's up to the

Belgian police now. . . . I'm surprised there's been no telegram yet to say he's been arrested in Brussels."

"Telegrams aren't delivered on Sunday after eleven. That is, unless you go to the post office and fetch them yourself. . . . What will you have, Inspector? . . . Do you know, people have been talking a lot about you in the town? . . ."

"Very nice of them!"

"No, I'm afraid they haven't been saying anything very nice about you. Your attitude has been interpreted as . . ."

"*Garçon! Un demi!*" called out Maigret. "And mind it's cold."

"You drink beer at this time of the day? . . ."

Marguerite passed along the street, and you could see from her walk that she was quite conscious of her reputation of being the best-dressed young lady in the town.

"They're a nuisance, these family scandals. . . . We haven't had a case of this kind in Givet for ten years. The last was a Polish workman who . . ."

"Excuse me, gentlemen. . . ."

Maigret dashed out into the street, just in time to catch Anna Peeters and her brother, who walked along with their heads high, as though to defy all the suspicion and animosity directed against them.

"Is it all right for me to come this afternoon, as I suggested yesterday?"

"Of course. At what time?"

"About half-past three, if that suits you."

With a sulky look on his face, he returned to his hotel, chose the most isolated table, and sat down to lunch.

"Put a call through to Paris, will you?"

"The telephone doesn't work after eleven on Sundays."

"All right. Never mind."

During the meal he scanned a little local paper. One of the headlines amused him!

The Givet Mystery Thickens.

If it had thickened for him, it had solidified altogether! In fact, there was no longer any mystery at all.

"Give me some more of those French beans," he called out to the waiter.

9
Round the Wicker Chair

OF all the little family rites that distinguished a Sunday in the Peeters' household, what most struck Maigret was the shifting of the wicker arm-chair.

During the week its place, and therefore the old man's, was by the kitchen stove. Even when visitors were received in the sitting-room, it made no difference.

But on Sundays, ritual demanded the old man's inclusion, and a place was set aside for the wicker chair by the window looking out onto the yard. The meerschaum pipe with the long wild-cherry stem lay on the window-sill by a jar of tobacco.

In a small leather-upholstered easy-chair Dr. Van de Weert sat with his legs crossed, facing the stove. He was reading the report of the Belgian pathologist, and as he read he nodded, shook his head, raised his eyebrows, or otherwise expressed whatever thoughts went through his mind.

Finally he handed the document back to Maigret. Marguerite, who was between them, wanted to take it, but her father objected:

"No, my dear. It's not for you."

Maigret handed it to Joseph Peeters.

"I dare say you'll be interested . . ."

They were sitting round the table: Joseph and Marguerite, Anna and her mother, the latter getting up every few minutes to see to the coffee. Like a true Belgian, the doctor was drinking Burgundy with his cigar, whose lighted end he waved constantly from side to side beneath his chin.

As he passed through the kitchen, Maigret had seen half a dozen tarts all ready.

"It's certainly a very thorough report," said the doctor, "though it doesn't say whether . . . whether . . ."

He glanced at his daughter with embarrassment.

"Whether she was raped," said Maigret bluntly.

And he nearly laughed aloud at the shocked expression on the little man's face. Not that he wasn't quite prepared to discuss the subject, but it had to be done in a suitably roundabout way.

"It would have been interesting to know," he went on. "For in cases such as these . . . there was one in 1911, for instance . . ."

And in duly veiled phraseology he described a very uninteresting case, to which Maigret did not bother to listen. Instead, he watched Joseph reading the pathologist's report.

It wasn't pretty reading either. A minute description of Germaine Piedbœuf's body in the state in which it had been found after long immersion in the water.

Joseph was pale. Like his sister Maria, he had rather pinched nostrils.

Would he stick it? Or would he give it a cursory glance and hand it back?

There was no doubt about the answer. He was reading it carefully line by line, and Anna, leaning over his shoulder, was reading too. He was about to turn over the page, when she stopped him.

"Just a moment."

She had still three lines to read. Then together they began the following page, which started with:

The hole in the cranium is of considerable dimensions, and no vestige of brain can be found within, it having been either washed out or eaten by fish.

"If you wouldn't mind taking your glass, *Monsieur le commissaire,* so that I can lay the table. . . ."

Madame Peeters removed the ash-tray, the box of cigars, and the decanter of schnapps, leaving them on the mantelpiece while she spread a hand-embroidered cloth over the table.

Anna and Joseph were still reading, while Marguerite eyed them enviously. The doctor, realizing that nobody was listening, returned to his cigar.

By the end of the second page, Joseph was white as a sheet, with dark shadows on either side of his nose, and beads of perspiration on his forehead. He had had enough, and it was Anna who turned over the page, and she alone who read to the end.

Marguerite left her seat and touched the young man on the shoulder.

"Poor dear! You shouldn't have read it. . . . Why don't you go outside for a breath of fresh air?"

Maigret pounced on the suggestion.

"That's a good idea. And I'd like to stretch my legs too."

A moment later they were both standing bareheaded on the quay. The rain had stopped. There was no space between the barges that was not exploited by some fishing enthusiast. A continuous electric bell, sounding somewhere beyond the bridge, signaled the opening of a cinema.

Joseph nervously lit a cigarette, then gazed out over the river.

"It's upset you, hasn't it? . . . Excuse my asking, but are you still thinking of marrying Marguerite?"

A long silence followed. Joseph avoided turning towards Maigret, who looked steadily at his profile. At last the young man turned his head, but it was towards the shop, then towards the bridge, and lastly back to the Meuse.

"I don't know."

"Have you ever been in love with her?"

"Why did you make me read that report?"

He passed his hand across his forehead, and in spite of the cold air his fingers were wet from the contact.

"Was Germaine much less pretty?"

"Oh, stop! . . . I don't know. . . . I've had it dinned into me all my life that Marguerite was beautiful, and intelligent, and cultured, and everything else. . . ."

"And now?"

"I don't know."

He didn't want to talk about it. The few words he spoke seemed to be dragged out of him against his will. He squeezed his cigarette so tight between his fingers that he tore the paper.

"She's prepared to go through with it, in spite of your son?"

"She wants to adopt it."

His features sagged. He looked ill with lassitude, or perhaps disgust. He shot a glance at Maigret to see if any more questions were coming.

"In your family everybody seems to think you'll be married soon. . . . Is Marguerite your mistress?"

The answer was a low growl:

"No."

"She wouldn't have it?"

"There was never any question of it. . . . I never dreamt of such a thing. . . . You don't understand."

And in sudden outburst:

"I've got to marry her. I've *got* to. And that's all there is to it."

The two men stared in front of them. Maigret began to feel cold without an overcoat. At that moment the shop door opened, and he once more heard the bell he knew so well. Then Marguerite's voice, too sweet, too caressing:

"What are you doing, Joseph?"

The young man's eyes met Maigret's for a second, and the look in them said yet more clearly:

"I've got to, and that's all there is to it."

And Marguerite went on:

"You'll catch cold if you stand out there much longer. Besides, the coffee's ready. . . . What's the matter? You're still as pale as a ghost. . . ."

Joseph turned towards the house, but not without a fleeting, wistful look towards the corner of the little street in which, invisible from where they stood, was the humble house where Germaine had lived.

Anna was already cutting the tarts into lavish slices.

*

Madame Peeters said little, as though conscious of the superiority of her children. But as soon as one of them spoke she smiled and nodded her approval.

All the same, she seemed to have made up her mind to say her little piece on this occasion.

"If you'll excuse me, *Monsieur le commissaire* . . . I hope I'm not going to say anything stupid. . . ."

To help herself out, she put another large slice of tart on the inspector's plate.

"I heard that certain things were found on board the *Etoile Polaire,* and also that Cassin had run away. . . . He's been here several times, but in the end I had to turn him away. First of all because he was always asking for credit, and then because he was never sober. . . . But that's not what I wanted to talk to you about. . . . The thing is, that if he's run away he must be guilty. And if he's guilty, that settles everything, doesn't it?"

Anna was placidly eating. She didn't look at Maigret or show any interest in her mother's theories. Marguerite was trying to coax Joseph to eat something.

"A small piece. . . . Just to please me. . . ."

With his mouth full, Maigret replied to Madame Peeters:

"I could answer your question if I was in charge of the case. But I'm not. . . . Don't forget: it was your daughter who asked me to come here to clear the family of suspicion."

Van de Weert fidgeted on his chair like a man who's dying to speak but can't get a word in.

"But really . . ." he began.

"Machère's in charge here, and . . ."

"But really, Inspector, there's such a thing as rank," said the doctor at last. "I don't know much about the police, but you must be a great deal higher up than he is."

"When I'm acting officially. But here I've no status at all. If I want to ask questions, people can refuse to answer. If I want to enter a house, they can refuse me admittance. . . . I went on board the *Etoile Polaire* at the risk of being turned away. By a stroke of luck I found the hammer Germaine was killed with, and the little coat she had been wearing. . . ."

"In that case . . ."

"In that case nothing! They're trying to arrest the man. Perhaps they've already done so by this time. Only, he may have quite a lot to say for himself. For instance, he might say that he picked the things up and kept them without realizing their importance. . . . Or he might say he was afraid to come forward. Having had a previous conviction, he thought nobody would believe him. . . ."

"That won't hold water."

"There's many a defense that won't hold water. But there's many a prosecution that's in exactly the same plight. . . . And as for prosecuting, there are others who might be accused. . . . Do you know what I was told today? . . . That Gérard Piedbœuf is in the devil of a mess and doesn't know how to get out of it. He's up to his ears in debt. Worse still, he was found pinching money from the cash-box. They were ready to overlook it, but they're withholding half his pay till it's all paid back."

"Really?"

"So why shouldn't he have got rid of his sister to claim damages from you?"

"What a dreadful idea!" exclaimed Madame Peeters, who was so horrified as to be unable to go on eating.

"You knew him pretty well, didn't you?" said Maigret, turning to Joseph.

"I saw a certain amount of him at one time. But it's a long time ago."

"Before the child was born, wasn't it? . . . You used to go on outings together, if I'm not mistaken. In fact, I think your sister went with you once, when you went to the Rochefort Caves. . . ."

"Did you really?" asked Madame Peeters, turning to Anna. "I never heard about that."

"If I did, I've forgotten all about it," said Anna, whose eyes were fixed on the inspector as she went on eating.

"Still, all that's of no importance," said Maigret. "As a matter of fact, I'm not sure what I wanted to say. . . . Anyhow, I'd like another piece of tart, Mademoiselle Anna. No, not the fruit one. I'll stick to your magnificent *tarte au riz*. You made it, I suppose?"

"She always does," Madame Peeters made haste to answer.

And suddenly a dead silence reigned in the room. Maigret said no more, and nobody else was disposed to undertake the burden of conversation. Nothing but the sound of munching all round the table. The inspector dropped his fork, and quickly stooping to pick it up, he caught sight of Marguerite's elegantly shod foot pressing on Joseph's.

"Machère seems to be a capable fellow," he said at last.

"He doesn't look very intelligent," said Anna slowly and deliberately.

And Maigret smiled at her. It was a smile of complicity.

"How many people do look intelligent? And when it comes to that, it's often just as well not to. As a rule, as soon as I've found a likely suspect, I take care to look as foolish as I can."

It was the first time Maigret had spoken to them like that. He seemed almost to be taking them into his confidence.

"But one can't really change one's features," said the doctor. "Take your forehead, for instance. To anyone with the least smattering of phrenology. . . . Well, I wouldn't mind betting you're very headstrong."

The meal came to an end at last. The inspector was the first to push back his chair and cross his legs. He took his pipe from his pocket and started filling it.

"Do you know what I'd like you to do, Mademoiselle Marguerite? Go to the piano and give us the *Song of Solveig*."

She hesitated and looked inquiringly at Joseph, while Madame Peeters murmured:

"She plays so well. . . . And such a voice!"

"There's one thing I regret, and that's that Mademoiselle Maria isn't with us. . . . And my last day too. . . ."

Anna looked sharply at him.

"Are you going?"

"This evening. . . . I have to work for my living, you know. Besides, my wife's getting impatient."

"And Monsieur Machère?"

"I don't know what he intends doing. But I suppose . . ."

The shop bell rang. There were hurried steps and then a knock on the door.

It was Machère in a state of great excitement.

"Is the inspector here?"

He hadn't seen him at once, taken aback as he was to find himself barging in on a family party.

"What is it?"

"I'd like a word with you."

"Excuse me, will you?"

And Maigret led the way into the shop, where he stood leaning on the counter.

"Those people make me sick."

Machère irritably jerked his chin in the direction of the sitting-room.

"The smell of their coffee and tarts is enough to turn me over, to start with."

"Is that what you came to tell me?"

"No. I've heard from Brussels. The train came in punctually . . ."

"But our bargee wasn't there!"

"You knew it already?"

"No, but I'm not surprised. Did you take the man for a fool? I certainly didn't. He must have got out at some little junction, taken another train, and then still another. . . . This evening he may be in Germany, or in Amsterdam, or he may even have doubled back to Paris."

"And where's he going to get the money from?" asked Machère sarcastically.

"What do you mean?"

"That I've been making inquiries. Yesterday Cassin couldn't pay for what was down on the slate in the *bistro,* so they refused to give him any more drinks. . . . And it's worse than that. It seems he owes money all round, and the tradesmen wanted to stop him sailing."

Maigret looked at his companion with an air of complete indifference.

"What else?"

"I didn't stop at that. And it's been the hell of a sweat on a Sunday, with half the people out. I even had to go to the cinema to question one or two."

While he smoked his pipe, Maigret amused himself putting weights in the two scale-pans to see if he could obtain a perfect balance.

"I found out that yesterday Gérard Piedbœuf borrowed two thousand francs. He got his father to sign an I O U, as no one would trust him that far."

"Did they meet?"

"Exactly! They did. It was a customs officer who saw Gérard Piedbœuf walking along the quay with Cassin, near the Belgian Customs House."

"At what time?"

"About two."

"Excellent!"

"What's excellent about it? If Gérard gave him the money, it was to . . ."

"Steady now! Don't jump to conclusions, Machère. It's a very risky business."

"The fact remains that Cassin, who hadn't a sou in the morning, could buy a railway ticket in the afternoon. I've been to the station. He paid for the ticket with a thousand-franc note. And it seems he had others."

"Others or *one* other?"

"I think he said others, though I'm not quite sure. . . . But tell me, what would you do in my place?"

"Me?"

"Yes."

Maigret sighed, knocked his pipe out against his heel, and pointed to the sitting-room.

"I'd go in and have a nice glass of schnapps. . . . Particularly as there's some music to go with it."

"Is that all you . . . ?"

"Come on! . . . You're not going to tell me you've anything else to do! . . . Where's Gérard Piedbœuf?"

"At the *Scala*. That's the cinema. With one of the factory-girls."

"I bet they're sitting in the best seats."

And Maigret, with a quiet chuckle, pushed the young detective into the sitting-room, where the light was failing sufficiently to blur all the outlines. A thin wisp of smoke rose straight up from the doctor's chair. Madame Peeters was taking the tea-things into the kitchen to wash up. At the piano, Marguerite was letting her fingers run casually over the notes.

"Do you really want me to play?"

"I do indeed. . . . Sit down, Machère."

Joseph was standing by the fire, with his right

elbow on the mantelpiece, staring through the window into the bleak gray light outside.

"L'hiver peut s'enfuir,
Le printemps bien-aimé
Peut s'écouler. . . .
Les feuilles d'automne
Et les fruits d'été
Tout peut passer . . ."

The voice lacked firmness. Marguerite had to make an effort to go on to the end. Twice she struck a false note.

"Mais tu me reviendras,
O mon beau fiancé,
Pour ne plus me quitter. . . ."

Anna was not in the room. Nor was she in the kitchen, where Madame Peeters could be heard creeping about, making as little noise as possible in deference to the music.

"Je t'ai donné mon cœur. . . ."

From the piano, Marguerite could not see Joseph's dejected figure. He had let his cigarette go out.

The room was darkening rapidly. The red-hot fire in the stove threw a purple glare onto the polished table-legs.

To Machère's amazement, Maigret slowly edged towards the door and slipped out, apparently unnoticed by the others. The young detective would have liked to know what he was up to, but he didn't like to interfere.

Maigret went upstairs without making a sound, to find himself on the landing facing two closed doors. It was almost quite dark here, but he could clearly see the two pale splodges which were the white china handles.

He paused for a moment, then put his pipe in his pocket, burning as it was, turned one of the handles, went in, and shut the door behind him.

Anna was there. The room was darker than the one downstairs. It seemed to be filled with a fine gray dust which lay thicker on the air in some places than in others, particularly in the corners.

Anna did not move. Hadn't she heard him enter?

She was looking out of the window across the darkening river. On the other bank lights had been lit which shot their pointed rays into the twilight.

From behind, Anna looked as though she was crying. She was tall. She seemed more powerful in build and more statuesque than ever.

Her gray dress melted in the gray light and made her part and parcel of her surroundings.

When he was only a step from her, one of the floorboards creaked, but still she did not move.

And then he put his hand on her shoulder, with quite surprising gentleness. At the same time he sighed like a man who no longer has to keep up appearances and can at last relax.

"Well! Here we are!"

She turned slowly round. She was perfectly calm. There wasn't a line which broke the severe harmony of her features.

Only the neck seemed slowly to swell a little as though from some mysterious inner pressure.

Every note of the music could be heard, and even the words of the *Song of Solveig.*

"Que Dieu veuille encore
Dans sa grande bonté
Te protéger. . . ."

Anna's pale blue eyes looked into Maigret's. A little pout heralded a sob, but it was quickly suppressed, and the line of the mouth fell back into the same quiet, statue-like repose as the rest of her.

10
The "Song of Solveig"

"WHAT are you doing up here?"

Strangely enough, Anna's tone wasn't aggressive. She looked sadly at him, and perhaps beneath the unruffled surface was fear. But no hatred.

"You heard what I said just now, didn't you? I'm leaving tonight. During these last few days we've been thrown into pretty close contact, you and I . . ."

He looked round him. At the big bed where the two girls slept, at the white bearskin mat, at the wallpaper covered with little pink flowers, at the wardrobe whose mirror no longer reflected anything but dusk and shadows.

". . . and I didn't want to go till I'd had it out with you."

The window was like a gray screen on which

Anna's silhouette grew darker and vaguer as the minutes went by. And all at once Maigret noticed a detail he had never noticed before. An hour earlier he couldn't have told you how she did her hair. Now he knew. In long close plaits which were rolled up in a large bun on her neck.

"Anna!" called Madame Peeters from the bottom of the stairs.

The music had stopped. Anna's and Maigret's absence had at last attracted attention.

"Yes. . . . I'm up here."

"Have you seen the inspector?"

"Yes. . . . We're coming. . . ."

To answer, she had moved over to the door. She closed it again, then came back towards Maigret, looking very grave, gazing at him with extraordinary intensity.

"What did you want to see me about?"

"You know as well as I do."

She didn't look away. She simply stood there, looking at him intently, with her hands clasped in front of her in an attitude that belongs to old women.

"What are you going to do?"

"I've already told you. I'm going back to Paris."

Then at last her voice quivered as she asked:

"And what about me?"

It was the first time she had betrayed her feelings. She was conscious of it herself, and it was no doubt to tide her over the moment that she walked over to the door again and switched on the light.

The lamp had a yellow silk shade which threw the light down into a small circle on the floor.

"First of all I must ask you a question," said Maigret. "Who put up the money? You had to act quickly and quietly, and I don't suppose you keep very much on the premises."

Maigret spoke slowly. The silence round them was absolute.

He paused, and once more looked about him, sensing all the atmosphere of this *petit bourgeois* house. At that moment it even seemed to him that he knew all that was going on downstairs. Dr. Van de Weert stretching his short legs out towards the stove; Joseph and Marguerite silently eyeing each other; Machère fidgeting irritably, longing to know what Maigret was doing; Madame Peeters picking up her knitting or filling up Machère's glass as she murmured politenesses.

And each time he glanced at her, the inspector found Anna's pale blue eyes fixed steadfastly upon him.

"It was Marguerite," she said at last.

"She has money of her own?"

"Yes. She was left some by her mother."

"She keeps it at home?"

"A few thousand francs, and a lot more in bearer bonds."

And Anna asked once more:

"What are you going to do?"

As she said it, tears came into her eyes. But

they disappeared so quickly that Maigret almost thought he'd been mistaken.

"And you?"

Why were they fencing like that? Why didn't they come straight to the point? Was each afraid of the other?

"How did you manage to bring Germaine Piedbœuf up to your room? . . . Wait a moment. . . . She came to the shop to ask news of Joseph and to fetch her monthly allowance. Your mother saw her first. Then you went into the shop. . . . Did you know then you were going to kill her?"

"Yes."

There was no feeling betrayed now, not even a little undercurrent of fear. The voice was clear and matter-of-fact.

"How long had you known?"

"About a month."

Maigret sat down on the big bed in which Anna and Maria slept. He passed a hand across his forehead, and studied the wallpaper which served as background to his adversary.

For there was no doubt about it: she was proud of what she had done. She took full responsibility. She almost vaunted its premeditation.

"So you love your brother as much as all that?"

But he knew it already. And it wasn't only the case with Anna. There were three women —no, four, with Madame Peeters—who adored the ground he trod on.

He wasn't good-looking. If you came to look critically at them, his features were all over the place. A long weedy figure, with a disproportionately long nose. Eyes that spoke volumes of boredom.

And yet, if he wasn't a god, he was the most beloved of mortals to his womenfolk, who would put their heads together in the parlor of the Flemish shop and extol his virtues.

"I was determined he shouldn't kill himself."

For a second, Maigret was on the point of losing his temper. He jumped up from the bed and started pacing up and down the room.

"Did he threaten to?"

"If he had married Germaine, he would have killed himself the same day. I know he would."

Maigret didn't know whether to laugh or swear. In the end he merely shrugged his shoulders. He thought of the talks he had had with Joseph. Joseph, not knowing which of the two girls he loved. Joseph, scared stiff by the thought of marrying either.

Yet to play up to his sisters, he tried feebly to play the part they'd given him.

"His life would have been ruined."

Of course it would! That is, if you looked at things from the standpoint of the *Song of Solveig*.

Mais tu me reviendras,
O mon beau fiancé. . . .

On the one hand, poetry, music, and fine sentiments.

On the other, the *beau fiancé*, with weak, blinking eyes and clothes that didn't fit him.

"Did you tell anyone about it?"

"Nobody."

"Not even your brother?"

"Least of all him."

"And you had been keeping the hammer hidden in your room for a whole month? . . . I see. . . . I'm beginning to understand."

He was also beginning to breathe heavily. For there was something peculiarly oppressive in this strange mixture of tragedy and petty meanness.

He found himself avoiding Anna's eyes as she stood there stock-still, gazing at him.

"You had to make a perfect job of it, because if you were found out, Dr. Van de Weert would never have allowed his daughter to marry Joseph. You thought over every possible weapon. A pistol would make a noise. Germaine never had meals here, so poison was out of the question. If your hands had been strong enough, I dare say you'd have strangled her. . . ."

"I thought of it."

"Don't interrupt! . . . You pinched a hammer from somewhere, for you weren't so stupid as to use anything belonging to the house. . . .

"On what pretext did you bring Germaine up here?"

And Anna answered almost casually:

"She'd been crying in the shop. She was always crying. . . . My mother had given her fifty francs towards her monthly allowance. I went out with her. I told her I could give her the rest. . . ."

"So you both came round in the dark and in by the back door. Maria was playing the piano, so nobody heard. You came upstairs. . . ."

Maigret looked at the door. And in a voice that he tried to keep steady he growled:

"You opened that door, and pushed her in front of you. . . . You got out the hammer . . ."

"No."

"What do you mean?"

"I didn't do it at once. In fact, I'm not sure that I should have had the nerve to do it at all . . . I don't know . . . if she hadn't said something. . . ."

Anna broke off for a moment, and then went on:

"She looked at the bed, saying: 'Oh! So that's where you and my brother used to . . . You've been cleverer than I have. You took good care not to land yourself with a baby.' . . ."

It was all so mean, so stupid, so squalid.

"How many blows?"

"Two. . . . She went down without a groan. I pushed her under the bed."

"Then you rejoined the others downstairs—your mother, Maria, and Marguerite—I suppose she'd come by that time? . . ."

"My mother was in the kitchen with my father. She was grinding the coffee for the following morning."

"Anna!" called Madame Peeters again. "Why don't you come? Monsieur Machère wants to go."

This time it was Maigret who went out and called down the stairs:

"Tell him to wait."

Then, returning to Anna:

"Did you tell Maria and Marguerite?"

"No. I knew Joseph would be coming. I couldn't move the body alone. But I didn't want anybody to see Joseph arriving. So I sent Maria to meet him on the quay and tell him to leave his motor-bike somewhere and slip in as quietly as possible."

"Wasn't Maria surprised?"

"She was frightened at once—too frightened to ask any questions. She simply did what she was told. I got Marguerite to the piano and asked her to sing. I knew we were bound to make a noise."

"You had already decided to put it in the tank on the roof?"

"Yes."

"So Joseph crept up here. What did he say when he saw the body?"

"Nothing. He couldn't understand. He stared at it, horrified, and it was all he could do to help me put it away."

To put it away! Upstairs. Through the little window in the loft. Dragged along over the slates and shoved into the galvanized iron tank!

Big beads of sweat stood out on Maigret's forehead.

"Of all the murderers I ever met . . ." he began.

But she interrupted him with:

"If I hadn't killed that woman, it would have meant Joseph's death."

"When did you tell Maria?"

"Never. . . . She didn't dare ask any questions. . . . Of course she suspected something, and that's what made her ill."

"And Marguerite?"

"I don't know. If she had any questions she succeeded in banishing them. You understand, don't you?"

Did he understand? Only too well! He understood the whole household, including Madame Peeters, who had gone on just as usual, suspecting nothing at all, and who could only be indignant at the slanderous suspicions of the townsfolk.

Including the old man, smoking or dozing in his wicker chair, oblivious even to the visits of the police.

And Joseph, coming to Givet as seldom as possible, leaving his sister to face the music. And Maria, returning home night after night from the convent in an agony of fear lest the worst had happened and the good name of the family was ruined forever.

"Why did you remove the body from the rain-water tank?"

"In the end it would have smelt. . . . I waited three days. Then on Saturday, when Joseph came, we took it down together and threw it in the river."

There were beads of sweat on her face too.

Not on her forehead, but on the down that covered her upper lip.

"Machère was suspicious of us from the start. When he seemed to be hot on the trail, I thought the only thing to do was to get a detective in on our side. . . . If only they hadn't found the body . . ."

"The case would have died a natural death," grunted Maigret. "Only, even without the body, there was Cassin, who had seen you throw it into the Meuse and had fished up the hammer and the coat. . . ."

He started pacing up and down the room. Wasn't Cassin more cynical than even a professional killer? He had known all along, but he had told the police nothing. At least, what he had told them he had told in such a way as to make it of no use to them. One moment he was lying. The next, he was hinting at the truth but pretending it was a lie.

To Gérard he had made out that he knew enough to humble the Peeters family once and for all. But there was a price: two thousand francs.

No sooner was he paid, however, than he went, not to the police, but to Anna. And this time there was a price too, and a much higher one.

Either she must cough up or he would go straight away and give the evidence Gérard had paid him for. If she did cough up, he would disappear and thus let suspicions fall on himself.

There was not enough money in the shop, and it was difficult for her to go out without attracting attention. So she had given Cassin a note for Marguerite, telling her she must at all costs provide what he asked.

Marguerite had paid, and had then run round to the Flemish shop, asking:

"What's the matter? . . . What's it all about?"

"Hush! . . . Joseph will be here in a moment. You'll soon be married now. . . ."

And the fluffy little fiancée had quickly effaced her suspicions.

That Saturday night they must all have breathed more freely in the Flemish house. The danger had passed. Cassin had gone, and so long as he wasn't caught all would be well.

"I suppose it was you who told Maria to sprain her ankle? You were afraid she would give the show away. . . ."

The air was oppressive, suffocating. Marguerite was playing again, but this time it was *The Count of Luxemburg*.

*

Did Anna realize what a monstrous thing she had done? There was no sign of it. She was perfectly calm. She simply stood there waiting, her pale blue eyes as clear as ever. Then, quite quietly, she said:

"They'll be wondering what we're doing."

"You're right. Let's go down."

But she did not move. Standing in the middle

of the room, she arrested him with a movement of her hand.

"What are you going to do?"

"I've told you three times," sighed Maigret. "I'm going back to Paris tonight."

"But what about . . . ?"

"The rest doesn't concern me. I wasn't sent here. If there's anything further you want to know, you must ask Machère."

"Will you tell him that . . . ?"

But Maigret had turned away and was already on the landing. Without answering, he walked downstairs, greeted once more by the all-pervading smell of the Flemish shop, with that trace of cinnamon which brought back old memories.

A bright line of light shone under the sitting-room door, whose panels picked up the vibrations of the music.

Maigret turned the handle and went in, astonished to find Anna on his heels, for he had not heard her follow him downstairs.

"What sort of a conspiracy have you two been plotting?" asked Dr. Van de Weert jokingly. He had just lit an enormous cigar, which he was sucking like a suckling baby.

"Please excuse us. Mademoiselle Anna was asking my advice about a journey that she seemed to be contemplating."

Marguerite had stopped playing as they came in.

"Are you really, Anna?" she asked.

"Oh, I'm in no hurry about it. But one of these days . . . "

Madame Peeters looked up from her knitting with a slightly uneasy look.

"I've filled up your glass, *Monsieur le commissaire*. I know you won't refuse another glass of our old Schiedam."

Machère, with puckered forehead, was trying hard to guess what had been going on.

As for Joseph, his face was flushed with the schnapps, of which he had drunk several glasses in quick succession.

"Would you like to do me a favor, Mademoiselle Marguerite? Will you play the *Song of Solveig* again—for the last time?"

And turning to Joseph:

"You turn over the pages for her."

It was sheer perversity on Maigret's part, like pressing on an aching tooth with the tip of one's tongue to make it ache the harder.

From where he was standing, his glass of Schiedam in his hand, his elbow on the mantelpiece, Maigret towered over the others—Madame Peeters leaning over the table within the glare of the lamp; Van de Weert smoking his cigar and stretching out his little legs; Anna standing against the wall.

And, at the piano, Marguerite playing and singing, with Joseph to turn over the pages.

The top of the piano was covered by a piece of embroidery on which stood a number of framed photographs: Joseph, Anna, and Maria at various ages from infancy upwards.

"Que Dieu veuille encore . . ."

But it was still Anna herself who engrossed Maigret's attention. For he could not resign himself to the idea that she had beaten him. He was hoping for something to happen, though he had no idea what.

At any rate he would have liked some sign from this woman who had called him to the rescue. Perhaps a quiver of the lips or a tear. Or she might leave the room precipitately, unable to face him any longer.

The first verse was over, and nothing had happened. Edging up to the inspector, Machère whispered:

"Are we staying much longer?"

"A few minutes."

As these words were exchanged, Anna watched them closely across the table, wondering whether some trap was being laid for her.

". . . pour ne plus me quitter . . ."

The last chords had hardly died out. Madame Peeters, her white head bent over her work, murmured:

"I've never wished any harm to anybody. . . . We're all in God's keeping. . . . It would have been a terrible thing if those two children . . ."

But she was too moved to go on. She wiped away a tear from her cheek with the stocking she was knitting.

And Anna still stood, quietly staring at Maigret. Machère was visibly losing patience.

"Come on," said the inspector. "You'll excuse our rushing off, won't you? My train leaves at seven. . . ."

Everybody stood up. Joseph's eyes flitted hither and thither, avoiding Maigret's above all. Machère groped for some suitable leave-taking and finally stammered:

"I must apologize for having suspected you. . . . But you'll admit that appearances . . . And if Cassin hadn't made off . . ."

"Will you show the gentlemen out, Anna?"

"Yes, Mother."

The three of them crossed the shop. It was locked up, being Sunday. But a tiny lamp, which shone on the brass scale-pans, was enough to show them the way.

Machère shook Anna's hand almost effusively.

"Once more . . . I'm so sorry. . . ."

For a few seconds Anna and Maigret eyed each other in silence. Then she muttered:

"You needn't worry. . . . I shan't stay here."

All along the quay, Machère never stopped talking, but Maigret only caught one or two snatches.

". . . now that we know who did it, I can go back to Nancy. . . ."

"I wonder what she meant?" thought Maigret. *"I shan't stay here. . . .* Will she really have the courage? . . ."

He looked at the Meuse, across which glittered the broken reflections of the lights on the other bank. One light, brighter than the others, came from the factory, where old Piedbœuf would later on be baking his potatoes in the cinders at the bottom of the stove.

They passed the little side-street. There was no light in the Piedbœufs' house.

11
The Last of Anna

"DIDN'T you bring it off this time?"

Madame Maigret was surprised to see her husband come home in such a bad temper. She felt the shoulders of his overcoat after helping him to take it off.

"You've been wandering about in the rain again. One of these days you'll go down with rheumatism, and then you'll be in a nice mess. . . . What was it all about? A murder?"

"A family affair."

"And that girl who came to see you?"

"Girl indeed! Give me my slippers, will you?"

"All right! Have it your own way! I won't ask any more questions! At least not on that subject. . . . Did you have decent meals at Givet?"

"Decent meals? I really don't know."

It was quite true. He had only the vaguest memories of what he'd eaten.

"Well, guess what I've made for you."

"*Guiches.*"

It wasn't very difficult, considering that the whole flat smelt of it.

"Are you hungry?"

"Yes, *ma chérie*. . . . And now, tell me all the news. There was no more bother about the furniture, I suppose?"

Why were his eyes constantly reverting to the same corner of the room, where there was an empty space? He was quite unconscious of it till his wife said to him:

"What's the matter? You seem to be looking for something."

Then he exclaimed out loud:

"Of course! The piano! . . ."

"What piano?"

"Nothing. You wouldn't understand. . . . Your *guiches* are marvelous. . . ."

"It wouldn't be much good being Alsatian if you couldn't make *guiches*. . . . Only, if you go on like that, there'll be precious little left for me. . . . Talking about pianos, the people on the fourth floor . . ."

*

A year later, Maigret entered the premises of a firm of exporters in the Rue Poissonnière. He had been summoned on the discovery of a forged banknote.

The showrooms were enormous and packed with goods, but the offices were small and unpretentious.

"I'll send for the note," said the head of the firm, ringing a bell.

Maigret's eye wandered, and he was vaguely conscious of a gray skirt approaching the desk. Beneath it were cotton stockings. Then he raised his eyes and gazed at the face that was bending over the desk.

"Thank you, Mademoiselle Anna."

The exporter saw Maigret's eye follow her out.

"She looks a bit fierce," he explained, "but you couldn't wish for a better secretary. She does just precisely the work of two: all the correspondence, and the accounts as well."

"Have you had her long?"

"Ten months."

"Is she married?"

"Oh, no! Far from it. That's her one little failing—a detestation of the masculine sex. One day a business acquaintance, who had come to see me, tried to take liberties, and she gave him just one look that fairly shriveled him up. You ought to have seen it. . . .

"She's here at eight o'clock sharp, if not earlier. And she's always the last to go. . . . I think she must be a foreigner, as she has a slight accent, but she's not the sort one asks a lot of questions . . ."

"Would you mind if I had a word with her?"

"By all means. I'll call her in again."

"No. I'd rather it was in her own room."

Maigret went through a glass-paneled door. A small office whose windows looked out onto a yard full of lorries. The whole house vibrated with the ceaseless flow of cars and buses along the Rue Poissonnière.

Anna was calm, calm as she had been when bending over her employer's desk, calm as he had always known her. Her age would now be twenty-seven, but anybody would have taken her for well over thirty. She had faded. There was no longer any freshness in her features or her complexion.

A few years more, and she would look middle-aged. A few more still, and she would look positively old.

"How's your brother?"

She looked away without answering, at the same time fidgeting with her blotter.

"Is he married?"

She merely nodded.

"Happy?"

At that word, the tears that Maigret had waited for a year ago came at last. Her throat swelled.

"He's taken to drink. . . . Marguerite's expecting a baby."

She threw the words at him, as though she held him personally responsible for everything.

"Is he getting on in his profession?"

"He set up on his own, but it wasn't a success. He's now taken a post in Rheims where he only gets a thousand francs a month. . . ."

She dabbed her eyes with her handkerchief, or rather jabbed at them furiously.

"Maria?"

"She died a week before taking the veil."

The telephone bell rang, and it was in another voice that Anna answered, as she automatically pulled a pad towards her and picked up a pencil:

"Yes, Monsieur Worms. . . . Certainly. . . . Tomorrow evening. . . . I'll cable them at once. . . . By the way, we've sent you a letter about that consignment of wool. I'm afraid there are one or two complaints. . . . No. I've no time now. It's fully explained in the letter. . . ."

She rang off. Her employer was standing in the doorway, looking from one to the other. The inspector returned with him to his room.

"What did I tell you? . . . Honest as the day, and as for competence. . . . You can tell in a moment, can't you?"

"Where does she live?"

"I can't give you her address offhand. But I know it's a women's hostel run by some society or other. . . . But . . . I'm beginning to be scared. Don't tell me you've had dealings with her already in your official capacity. I shouldn't care very much about having a secretary who'd been mixed up in anything criminal. . . ."

"You needn't worry," answered Maigret slowly. "It wasn't in my official capacity."

And then more briskly:

"Now! About this note—you found it . . ."

But as he listened to the exporter's story he had one ear pricked for the sounds in the next room. She was telephoning again.

"No, monsieur. He's engaged at the moment. This is Mademoiselle Anna speaking. I think I can tell you anything you want to know. . . ."

Gustave Cassin of the *Etoile Polaire* was never heard of again.